RHYMES FOR
LEARNING TIMES

RHYMES FOR LEARNING TIMES

Let's Pretend Activities for Early Childhood

by Louise Binder Scott

Publishers
T. S. DENISON and COMPANY, INC.
Minneapolis, Minnesota

T. S. DENISON & COMPANY, INC.

Standard Book Number: 513-1763-1

Library of Congress Catalog Card Number: 73392

Printed in the United States of America
Copyright © 1983 by T.S. Denison & Co., Inc.
Minneapolis, Minn. 55431

TABLE OF CONTENTS

THE AUTHOR

Louise Binder Scott (Ed. M., Boston University; former speech-language-hearing-reading specialist, San Marino Schools, California; Associate Professor of Speech Education, California State University (at Los Angeles) is author of many publications. She is co-author with J.J. Thompson of *Rhymes for Fingers and Flannelboards,* a book which has been used widely by teachers of primary children, and by the Canadian Broadcasting Company in its children's programs.

Other publications include *Phonics in Listening, Speaking, Reading and Writing; Talking Time* (with J.J. Thompson); *Learning Language Skills,* a language program for primary grades; *Language Experiences for Young Children; Singing Fun* and *More Singing Fun* (with Lucille F. Wood); *Mathematical Experiences for Young Children* (with Jewell Garner); *Time for Phonics* and *A New Time for Phonics.* She has written stories for many recordings, and has also produced many filmstrips for stories, language and phonics.

Sources and Acknowledgements

The author wishes to acknowledge the following as sources of material used in this book:

Olive M. Amundson, Teacher of Bilingual Children, Pico Rivera, California.

Talking Time, 1951 and 1968 editions, for poems written by the author.

Traditional rhymes, where no author has been located and which appear in many anthologies and other books.

The author wishes to thank Deanna Durr Clark, M.A. (Orientation and Mobility Specialist, Los Angeles County Schools, Los Angeles, California), a consultant who used many of these materials with her classes.

All rhymes and creative materials are the original works of Louise Binder Scott unless otherwise specified.

FOR THOSE WHO USE THIS BOOK

Rhymes for Learning Times is intended for classroom teachers of children in preschool and kindergarten through grade two; for parents; and for aides and paraprofessionals who assist the teacher. The rhymes may also be used by teachers of speech and by those working with physically handicapped children and others enrolled in special education classes.

Many of the rhymes in this book involve the use of the whole body, but can be modified for fingers only, if circumstances indicate such modification. There are rhymes designed for rote and rational counting and for the operations of addition and subtraction. Other rhymes are effective for relaxation, for body orientation and spatial relationships, for integration with subjects being taught, for appreciation of seasons and holidays, for dramatizations, and for vocabulary enrichment.

Rhymes for Learning Times has a wide range of use. The simpler and shorter selections will be enjoyed by preschoolers. Most rhymes are adaptable to kindergarten use, while longer ones demanding full body action or reading from a duplicated sheet will interest second, third, and even fourth graders. Those dealing particularly with seasons and holidays will make attractive wall charts.

THE HISTORY OF THE FIRST ACTION RHYME

Action rhymes where fingers are used as "characters" and given personalities, and where counting is predominant can be traced to Indian lore before Columbus arrived in North America. In the Rome of 50 A.D., children played "Bucca, bucca, quot sunt hic", meaning "How many fingers do I hold up?" A manuscript dated 1364 refers to the nursery rhyme "Here Sits the Lord Mayor." This rhyme holds as much appeal today as it did over six hundred years ago. The same fourteenth century manuscript tells us that toes were tweaked in "This Little Pig Went to Market" and the foot was patted in "Shoe a Little Horse."

The action rhymes we recall best had their inception over a century ago with Friedrich Froebel, who is considered the "father of the kindergarten" and who opened the first education center in Blankenburg, Germany in 1837. During the years 1851-60, the Prussian government banned what it called "a dangerous institution," the kindergarten, as socialistic. People were incensed by the decree. They ignored it and kindergartens flourished.

While walking in the woods, Froebel thought of the name "child garden" where children are cultivated in accordance with the laws of their own being, of God, and of nature.

To Froebel, psychology was unknown, yet his writings indicate sound understanding of this discipline. To him, the democratic responsibilities of group life were basic. He maintained that the chief core of the curriculum was the child. In order to understand children, he studied their early impressionable years when individual habits, attitudes, and abilities are usually established, and when the art of working together could be considered a permanent way of learning. Froebel took the games and songs of the people and adapted them to the child's education. He saw an opportunity to integrate the meanings and the emotional satisfaction of seeing relationships of part to part and part to whole. He believed that children should be children and not be expected to be miniature adults, and that all education must have a sense of perception basis. He felt that children should be taught from objects which are known in their own setting. In his kindergarten, Froebel encouraged children to build concepts out of their interests and out of the world around them. His theory was that *play* was the most effective tool for learning and he was the first teacher to create and use concrete and structural materials for children. Mathematics was one of the most important means for developing number concepts in the preschool child's mind.

"The Mother Play", as Froebel called the activity that involved mother, child, and a finger play, was a part of the primitive source from which sprang the folk tale, the ballad, and the fable, and as a literature it has survived just as all good literature survives. The rhymes are not like the works of Grimm who collected tales and set them down with precision. Froebel used folk lore, it is true, but he transfigured it with his own ideas. He brought into his verses the childlike, spontaneous, and natural quality of the child's language.

In 1873, *Mother Plays and Nursery Songs with "Notes to Mothers"* by Friedrich Froebel was published. Here is a sample of a rhyme appearing on page 61 of that book:

What's this? What's this? What's this?
This is the little thumb round
Like a little plum round.
And this? and this? and this?
This little finger points the place,
And straight it is yet bends with grace.
And this? and this? and this?
This finger doth the longest show;
And makes the middle of the row.
And this? and this? and this?
This one the golden ring shall wear,
And like the gold is pure and fair.
And this? and this? and this?
This finger is the least of all,
And just completes the number small.
Oh, yes! Oh, yes! Oh, yes!
It is! It is! It is!
And though these little gifts have such a part to fill,
They're all together bound and governed by one will.

In *Finger Plays* by Emelie Poulson, published in 1893, we find many of the same finger plays appearing in collections today. Examples are:

Right hand: Here is a beehive. Where are the bees?
                    Hidden away where nobody sees.
                    Soon they come creeping out of the hive,
                    One! two! three! four! five!

Left hand: Once I saw an anthill
                    With no ants about.
                    So I said, "Dear little ants,
                    Won't you please come out?"
                    Then as if the little ants
                    Had heard my call,
                    One! two! three! four! five! came out!
                    And that was all.

ACTION RHYMES PROVIDE
A WORLD OF MAKE-BELIEVE

Childhood is a time of wonderment, curiosity, and investigation. Each day, a secret gate leading into a garden of sensory images and challenges opens to exciting adventure with experiences and with words.

Deprived of play, there may be little chance for a child to observe and grow through insight. Children may never reach adolescence prepared to assume adult roles when they lack activity where they can pretend to be people in an adult world. It is an accepted theory that favorable play conditions in childhood foster creativity and initiative in adult life. In early childhood education, play is recognized as a *means of self teaching.* Through play, children develop ways of learning. They gain a favorable self-concept, for they can express freely and carry their experiments through in constructive ways, control their primitive emotions, and gain satisfaction in their own abilities. Eventually, they can attain a basis for abstract thinking and spatial relationships, and can converse and share with others.

Studies have been made of the play habits of animals. The young kitten, the puppy, the colt, and the goat are playful, while the chicken is settled. Generally, the higher the intelligence of a species, the more it indulges in play.

Intellectual interests are a necessary part of play.
Everything children do provides situations from which they learn. Obviously, they are unaware of the significance of their own play. They do not realize that it provides the means whereby they can cope with stresses of everyday existence and that it fulfills many purposes in their young lives.

Play and Fantasy

> The people I feel sorry for
> Have never heard a dragon roar.
> They've never looked out on the lawn
> To try to find a leprechaun.
> They've lived their lives all by themselves
> By never knowing sprites or elves.

The ability to play out in fantasy solves many inner conflicts with feelings of love, hate, hostility, aggression, and anger. At the same time, children build up, through experience with play, their ideas about reality and their understanding of self in the world in which they find themselves.

The task of learning to fit in with adult standards of behavior, which young children often find bewildering, is a very exacting one to which society keeps pressing them to conform. In order to develop emotionally and remain mentally healthy, children should be given opportunities to perform adult tasks in substitute form.

Play is Serious Business.
We may say that all play is serious and totally absorbing. Some is real, while some may be pretense. Elkind said that it requires experience and sensitivity on the part of teachers and parents to recognize what is *reality* to a child and what is *fantasy.* He explains that what may appear to be fun and games really is serious work to a small child whose play prepares him or her for mental development. "Critics stress the fact that all play has mental and creative components."[1] Shifting from fantasy to reality is extremely difficult to define. We cannot tell a child that his or her fantasies are not true, yet we can lead him/her toward understanding of reality without inhibiting his/her fertile imagination.

[1]David Elkind, Ph.D., *Pen,* Vol. 1, No. 4, May/June, 1970.

THE PARENTS AND ACTION RHYMES

Finger plays and action rhymes have descended through the ages and are found in most countries of the world. Their perpetuation appears to be due to the physical and close contact of the parent-child relationship in which the family is involved.

A second German edition of *Mother Plays,* which was published over a century ago, referred to the mother-child relationship as being the strongest influence in the child's learning.

Although the language describing the parent's role is flowery and elaborate, the messages hold true, for the parent tends the child, cuddles it, sings to it, and strives to open its mind to the environment. The parent touches each tiny finger and toe and awakens the mind to objects in contact with the body, to human life, to animals, to community, and to nature. The body contact with the parent from the day of birth is of great importance, and parents serve as models for language formation.

As the child sits on the parent's lap, the mother or father recites simple repetitive rhymes, tweaks each finger and toe, guides the little hands to various parts of the body and helps clap out the rhythm of words which often are not understood at all, nor need they be explained.

The mother and father will find many of the simple rhymes in this book to be of quieting and enriching influence. They will help build the child's self-confidence and will instill feelings of belonging in the family group and which for the child will gradually enlarge to school and community.

MOVEMENT IS A NATURAL MEANS
OF SELF-EXPRESSION

In creative action, we note the complete absorption and concentration that goes into the form of dramatization and identification with which a child plays a role. For the time being, he/she is asked to be a growing seed, a carpenter, or a duckling. Rhythm, repetition, and rhyme characterize all that is created in movement and sound.

The action rhymes in this book accentuate movement.
Movement is the first and most natural means of self-expression and is said to be the basis for all drama. At first, actions are purely physical, but eventually the child *imitates* and then relives creatively the experiences of animals and people.

Action rhymes create an awareness of body parts and their movements.
The young child discovers body parts and what they can do in relation to space. Movement and life are inextricably related. From the earliest hours of life, a child explores the body's capacity for movement. The form of exploration is fun, yet it also is the child's main channel for releasing emotions. As a result of exploration, a child builds an image of the body which provides a means of orientation in space. Children perceive themselves in relation to objects and people around them and the spaces in between. In this way, a sense of direction is created. They learn that movements in action rhymes vary in speed and fluency and so are aware that the body can take on different shapes, such as stretching toward the sky, turning around, crouching down, standing tall, or being completely relaxed. Words themselves stimulate movement. The teacher suggests: "Your head rolls around like a rubber ball" or "You are a little seed growing up from the ground." An important means of understanding things in childhood is by identifying with the object or person under consideration. The child does not merely *pretend* to be a squirrel. He/she *becomes* the squirrel.

"In the earliest years, children do three important things with the body. They *bend*, *stretch*, and *twist*, and these three basic movements provide the foundation for the full range of their skills. Energy, speed, and balance become important to movement and a child must learn to control them."[2] Movement facilitates language development, but it has its own language as well. It activates the imagination, evokes moods, and stimulates creative energy.

Action rhymes promote teamwork.

In this form of play, children meet other children their own age who are similarly occupied. They learn to recognize that their needs do not necessarily coincide with the needs of others in the group. By now, the child likes being with other children and is becoming aware that he/she is not the center of the group. Eventually, common interests emerge out of this group play, and action rhymes are one of the group or social activities that leads to teamwork later on.

Action rhymes stimulate listening skills.

They help a child to wait for a turn, to share with others, and to discern and identify words that rhyme. Often a young child will teach the rhyme to a younger brother or sister and thus create an ideal carry-over from school to home.

Action rhymes emphasize oral language and speech improvement.

The rhymes facilitate verbal and self-expression. Although the activities in this book vary, they are easy to interpret. The language is simple. The child learns how to phrase, and vocal inflections are improved because of the dramatic content. No one is alone. Every child has an opportunity to speak with others in a group situation. Here a child has a chance to put words together to complete a sentence or thought. Many of the rhymes contain such sounds as "th" (voiced) in *this*, "th" (voiceless) in *three* and *thumb*, "s" in *see, six,* and *seven*, "r" in *run* or *ran*, and "f" in *four* and *five*. Children with substandard speech may omit plurals (such as "three cat" for "three cats") and various endings. They sometimes confuse tenses and omit apostrophes. These children, too, will find help through the use of the repetition and group activity these rhymes afford.

Action rhymes help the bilingual child.

These children learn new sounds their native language does not contain, such as the schwa "a" in *around*, the "sh" and "ch" sounds which are confused in usage, as well as the many vowels which do not occur in their own language.

Often with Spanish-speaking children, teachers will use idiomatic expressions such as: "Little Miss Muffet sat on a tuffet." Nonsense words will provide speech and rhythmic experiences even though the children may not understand meanings.

Action rhymes serve as an excellent directional medium.

Children must listen carefully to know what to do next with fingers and bodies. Sharp eyes are needed, for they must not only watch the leader (in most cases the teacher) to note what to do next, but also must be aware of their own bodies to see if they are following the play correctly. Yet all action should not be imitative. The child must be given an opportunity to create his or her own movements, else all action will become automatic and enforced.

Action rhymes can help the physically handicapped child.

They can be used by much older children who have difficulty with coordination. Simple finger manipulations can be of great help to a brain-injured child who has difficulty in controlling movements. Children with coordination difficulties can be assisted in simultaneous control of memory, voice, eye, and body movements.

[2]Alice Yardley, *Senses and Sensibility* (Evens Brothers; London, England; 1970), p. 89.

If this child is severely handicapped, it will be helpful to place pictures or objects on a table. The child can then touch each one and say, "This little ball."

Action rhymes help a child to coordinate muscles in progressive movements.

Small muscle movement strength is needed for writing, tracing and drawing, and large muscle movement for whole-body action.

Action rhymes help the slow learner.

Slow learners fear making mistakes. Through action rhymes, they may begin to act and speak simultaneously, which can be quite an achievement. Little by little they will be able to memorize simple lines, coordinate body actions, and experience success. The child's inability to understand what to do may be that he/she cannot think of the *whole* and *parts of the whole* at the same time. The slow learner may discover abstractions such as words connected with time, size, and dimension. These children (or any children) develop the skill of saying lines with the teacher without fully realizing what he or she has accomplished. It is advisable to begin a rhyme by having the students echo the teacher or repeat the words after her/him until they become simultaneous and spontaneous expression.

Action rhymes help develop a readiness for reading.

Better listening habits and learning to follow directions are established. Auditory discrimination is strengthened. Some of the lengthier rhymes can be duplicated for more mature children who can read, used for choral speaking, or written on wall charts. Placing pictures illustrating a rhyme on a flannelboard and asking the child to "read" pictures instead of words will be helpful.

Emphasized are values such as understanding rhythm, ability to reason and conceptualize, promotion of social growth, and learning a new language. Many of the action rhymes in this book tie in with subject matter—seasons, community workers, holidays, and other categories described in the subject index.

Action rhymes provide the child with a positive self-concept and emphasize ego strength.

They also help the teacher court the child's self-confidence. The child, when performing, has someone to play with, listen to, and contact—all important to this stage of child development.

Action rhymes help a child to think in orderly fashion.

The rhymes create orderliness in their succession of events and prompt the child to think sequentially.

The action rhyme is only a make-believe beginning.

The rhymes in this book are extended to situations that interest children, one reason why an expansion of the rhyme into other learning activities is advised. Children need to understand relationships which exist between themselves and the circus or farm which they have recently "played." An alert teacher will satisfy those needs by presenting rhymes in a way that will encourage not only initiative, but also independent action, thinking, and verbalization.

ACTION RHYMES AND MATHEMATICS

Most children come to school having reached a second step in the understanding of what it means to "count", when number names are connected to objects in a more or less conventional sequence. Tallying is an operation when a one-to-one correspondence is made between objects in a group and number names. Of course, the young child is not considering a total in any sense, such as "four plus four is eight," but simply is giving all objects or animals names just as he or she might indicate size, as "big one" and "little one," or color, "red one" or "blue one."[3]

It is well worth making sure that kindergarten children thoroughly familiarize themselves with the correct order of numbers, both cardinal and ordinal. Children already are knowledgeable about numbers in the sense that they are picked up by a participating child in connection with birthdays, numbers of fingers and toes, one knife and one fork for each person, sharing something equally, and adding to or subtracting from sets.

Contrary to some thought, these action rhymes do not teach children to count on their fingers. In following the teacher's movements, the child will forget that fingers are fingers, but rather they will represent insects, animals, and people to him/her.

SUGGESTIONS for TEACHING FINGER PLAYS and ACTION RHYMES

1. The action rhyme or finger play for a preschool, kindergarten, or even first grade child should be brief. A few verses are more effective than many, else the child is robbed of the joy of mastery.

2. Be sure that all children are ready for participation. If the rhyme concerns several different animals on a farm or in a zoo, have a short relaxation period first. If attention wanes, change the activity, for the rhyme may be too long and too complicated for one age group and may need to be used with children who are more mature or are able to read.

3. When facing a group, mirror the action you wish the children to perform. If a child uses the right hand, hold up your left (which appears to be the right hand to the child). Movements have to be made in reverse of those expected of the group.

4. Be aware of left-handedness. Left-handed children may perform right-handed movements in an awkward manner. If you sense a coordination problem, ask the child to stand beside you and watch your actions. Some of the rhymes switch from right to left hand rather rapidly. Say the lines very slowly at first so that the children understand directions before quickening the pace.

5. If the rhyme contains several different characters, read it slowly to the class. Perform the actions as you do so. Then point out clearly which lines the children can help you say without prodding them. Mumbling children struggling for words can be frustrating for both children and teacher. Children need a precise idea of what they are to do in a group activity. At first, they may say only words that are easy to recall at the ends of lines or three or four words at the beginning.

6. Use the same rhyme several times before going on to another. Children enjoy repeating familiar lines. They like repetitive words that give them speaking security when used in rhythmic context. Compile a list of rhymes certain children enjoy so that they can choose from their repertory.

7. Avoid a didactic approach such as "Do this with me now," or using a commanding tone of voice. Say instead, "If we say this, we will have fun," or "Let's all do this. I think we will enjoy it."

[3]Louise Binder Scott and Jewell Garner, *Mathematical Experiences for Young Children* (McGraw-Hill, New York, 1978).

8. It is inadvisable to request that children perform actions such as dramatizing or pantomiming without sufficient instruction or motivation. Rather than describe certain movements you expect them to make, occasionally ask "How would you hop if you were a toad? Show us." Draw from the children their own ideas of movement. If all children were instructed to jump in the same way, creative purposes would be defeated.

9. If you feel that children are capable of reading lines without frustration, type or write the words for them to say. Some of the rhymes lend themselves to one-line-a-child, which is quite effective for programming purposes.

10. If asked to draw pictures or construct puppets, you may run into coordination problems or a time element. Plant the "seeds," but allow the ideas to emanate from the child. Ask, "Do you think that pictures for the flannelboard could be made? Would a stick puppet make a good character for this rhyme? Are there other ways we could use this rhyme?"

11. If children have articulation or foreign language problems, rather than single out a particular child who may be saying *dis* for *this*, write the correct word on the board: *this*. Say, "I put the tip of my tongue out when I say *this*. Try it with me. Can you make your tongue tip work? *This.*" Then repeat the rhyme that begins: "This little kitten..." Refer children with speech problems that require special help to a speech-language specialist.

12. If a child is reticent and silent, ask that child to sit beside you or with two or three other children close to you and encourage him/her to follow your finger or body movements. Some children do not like to be touched and may shy away from your guiding hand. Occasionally, sit in the background and encourage individuals to be leaders as they choose their favorite action rhyme to perform with the class.

13. Encourage talk, talk, talk! Oral communication is very important. Ask questions that will elicit oral responses and reasoning. For example, ask "How would you find a worm if you were a bird?" rather than saying, "The little bird found a worm in the ground," and ending the selection with a mere memorized line.

14. Rhyming words are a part of rhythm. Without those words, there would be no rhymes to play and say. Make the most of these words by asking occasionally for words in the selection that rhyme. Say part of a line and suggest that children complete it.

RELAXATION IS IMPORTANT

Many young children live in an environment of confusion and noise. Increased tension due to complicated economic and social structures have resulted in great stress being placed upon a child's nervous system.

Teachers should make every effort in the classroom to help their pupils feel a sense of well-being. Since many children are conditioned to loud noises, it may be difficult for them to experience feelings of quiet. They occasionally need to feel sensations of repose in order to make full use of concentration.

A calm, unhurried teacher and a room where children are able to think is indeed an uplifting place. It should be the object of all education to work for a relaxed atmosphere where children can feel free from tension as they learn and create.

Many of the rhymes in this book serve these purposes.

THE NURSERY RHYME AND MOTHER GOOSE

Mother Goose rhymes, although recommended, have been omitted from this book for they can be found easily in other publications. They make effective finger plays and action rhymes and are used for this medium in most preschool and primary centers.

Mother Goose rhymes with which we are most familiar originated in England. They furnish excellent material for starting children with unfamiliar action rhymes. Young children will not know of the origin or purposes of the English rhymes, and some of the references and terminology will not be understood, but the rhymes themselves provide a fascination of rhythm and action for all primary children.

Recommended books containing nursery rhymes from different countries:

Alastair Reed and Anthony Kerrigan, *Mother Goose in Spanish.* (Thomas Y. Crowell, New York, 1968).

Antonio Fransconi, *The House That Jack Built.* (Harcourt, Brace, and Company, New York, 1958). Spanish and English.

Charlotte B. De Forest, *The Prancing Pony, Nursery Rhymes From Japan.* (Walker/Weatherhill, New York, 1967).

Henry Carrington Bolton, *The Counting-Out Rhymes for Children.* (D. Appleton and Company, New York, 1888).

Iona and Peter Opie, *The Oxford Nursery Rhyme Book.* (Oxford University Press, New York, 1955).

Patricia Fent Ross, *The Hungry Moon.* (Alfred A. Knopf, New York, 1946). Spanish and English.

J.R. Monsell and Humphrey Milfoed, *Polechinella, On Nursery Rhymes of France.* (Oxford University Press, London, 1928).

Modern Mother Goose:

Raymond Briggs, *The Mother Goose Treasury.* (Coward McCann, Inc., New York, 1966).

Marguerite De Angeli, *The Book of Nursery and Mother Goose Rhymes.* (Doubleday, Garden City, New York, 1954).

USING VARIETY

After a child is familiar with a rhyme, variations can be introduced such as: a line-a-child, using puppets or flannelboard figures, painting, selecting items from the odds and ends box to create masks, costumes, and encouraging dramatization such as adding new characters. For example, if there are five ducks, children may wish to extend the number and tell what additional ducks are doing. Forget the rhyming aspects. At all times, children should be invited to make up their own rhymes. Write them down and make a book of them. If you are a second or third grade teacher, consider using some of the rhymes for wall charts, particularly those that deal with seasons or holidays.

Many of the rhymes center around one character where part of the selection can be used one day and additional parts the next. If the rhyme is in complete story form which contains several episodes, it will be helpful to duplicate a copy for more advanced children and ask volunteers to read certain lines or stanzas. Some of these "story rhymes" can be used for special programs at Halloween, Hanukkah, Christmas, or Thanksgiving.

HOW PARENTS AND AIDES CAN HELP

At the first part of the year, ask room helpers to put in a call for magazines or discarded books from which colorful pictures can be obtained. Go through the books and list pictures that will be needed for the rhymes so that the helpers can cut them out and mount them. Buy pattern books with line drawings and duplicate them so that a dozen or so of the same figure can be colored, cut out by children, and backed with flocked paper, smooth sandpaper, or outing flannel bits. Children should be encouraged to draw and color their own pictures for their favorite rhymes.

THE JOY OF DRAMATIZATION

Young children are all involved in "acting" in the traditional sense, but the experience will not be stimulating if the child is instructed in every motion to make and in how to express every word. Each child should be able to participate at his/her own level and involve the imagination.

Asking "How do you think the giant would talk and walk?" can bring varieties of responses and giant imitations from children.

"Pretend you are a clown. What would a clown do? Show us. Have you seen a clown? Where? Describe a clown. Does a clown look different from a person at the check stand in a supermarket? How? If you wanted to look like a clown, what would you do to your face? What kind of clothes would you wear? Here is a poem I will read one line at a time. Show me what you would do to make us believe you are a clown. Who will be clowns?" (Select three or four children.)

> A clown has a funny, funny walk.
>
> A clown smiles and she waves her hand
>
> A clown nods her head from left to right.
>
> A clown plays a flute in the band.

"Did everyone act like a clown in the same way? Show us how you would walk, Gary. Show us a different walk, Ruth. Let's pick five clowns and watch them."

> A clown bends from side to side.
>
> A clown dances with big feet.
>
> A clown looks very, very sad.
>
> A clown likes lollipops to eat.

"Did every clown do the same thing in the same way?"

Eliciting Verbal Responses

Statement   What do you like about a clown? (Response.)

How can a clown make you laugh?

Command	Bozo is a clown. If you want Bozo to do a trick, what would you say to Bozo? (Response)
Question	Ask Bozo what he/she likes to eat. (Response)
	Ask Bozo how he/she makes up his/her face.
Exclamation	Say something to let us know you are surprised. Bozo gives you a balloon. Bozo invites you to the circus.

MAKING VOICES WORK

The children enjoy using their voices to express emotion. Try these suggestions by asking a child to:

Look sad and say, "My puppy is so sick."

Look sleepy and say, "I'm tired and I want to go to bed."

Look angry and say, "You stepped on my kite!"

Look sympathetic and say, "I'm sorry. I didn't mean to step on your kite."

Look scared and say, "A car is coming! Look out!"

When asking for these kinds of vocal responses, be sure to express yourself softly so that no one will be inclined to imitate you.

Although everyone may recite a rhyme in unison and act it out, be sure that children have turns occasionally at saying lines singly and making decisions as to which motions should be made.

"This rhyme is about a turtle. How would a turtle walk? How would you show with your hands a turtle with a shell on its back?

"This rhyme is about some dinosaurs. As I say a line, act as a dinosaur would act."

These suggestions will help give the rhymes in this book variety. Even though hand and body movements are included, discuss the rhyme first by asking questions such as, "Show us how a snowman (or lady) would melt to the floor without making a sound. Show us how a seed would grow up out of the ground and make a sunflower. Make believe your fingers are lighted candles. Blow out the lights on each candle. How would a scarecrow scare a crow? How would snowflakes fall from the skies?"

Have fun with the rhymes!

Rhythm is facilitated when young children are aware of movement. There is movement and sound all around them in everyday life—the thump, thump of jumping rope, running feet, Daddy walking up the steps, and someone knocking on the door. Children associate sounds with the movements that make them. They also are aware that music is made of rhythm and sound from the time they sing "Pat-a-cake, pat-a-cake, Baker Man." When the child claps, there is rhythm.

Many speech rhythms and finger plays in this book can be formulated into elementary melodic work. You can "sing" the words and ask children to echo them.

Clap your hands: clap, clap, clap.

Tap your fingers: tap, tap, tap.

19

Slap your knees: slap, slap, slap

Close your eyes and take a nap.

You may sing instructions and clap:

Sit up tall; sit up tall;

Sit up tall and listen.

Sing and clap until the children learn echoing. Once they have grasped the rhythm, take direction to body parts:

Tap your feet with a very slow beat:

Tap, tap, tap!

Tap your feet with a very fast beat:

Tap, tap, tap, tap, tap.

Encourage children to sing requests:

"May I have a turn? I want to play with blocks."

Extend the activity to different movements:

"Teach-er, teach-er, may - I - have - a turn."

When arriving at this stage of asking questions or making statements such as, "I have a birthday next week" in song, the children will have plenty of practice and feel secure with echoing, singing, or even making up simple rhythms. Ask, "How many fingers are on each hand?" The child sings, "I have five fingers on each hand." The class may repeat, "Arthur has five fingers on each hand." Extend the song.

I have five fingers on each hand.

They all belong to me.

I can make them do things,

As anyone can see.

Ask, "What can your fingers do?" A child replies in song. Sorting out words and saying or singing them rhythmically can be linked with anything done in the classroom or what is happening at home.

BODY MOVEMENT SUGGESTIONS

Body movements are planned to help children move smoothly and safely through space and to effect the high levels of control so necessary for fine coordination skills.

The following whole-body activities will be enjoyed by children at times throughout the day. They can be used with only fingers and hands as well as encompassing the whole body.

balancing like a cat walking along a fence (Halloween)
bending like a tree branch in a brisk wind, then a breeze
hopping like birds looking for worms
fluttering gracefully like butterflies
chasing your tail like a puppy
crawling like a mouse into a hole; *crawling* to steal cheese
creeping like a caterpillar and making a bumpy motion

20

climbing up a tree; a ladder; over a wall
dancing on tiptoes like a wound-up doll or clown
dancing like elves on the lawn
flopping in the wind like a scarecrow
falling leaves in autumn
galloping or *trotting* like a pony
hopping like a toad or a rabbit
jumping like a grasshopper or cricket
curling up like a sleepy kitten
scampering like mice
putting presents under a tree like Santa
rocking on a rocking horse or back and forth
running like a beetle
skating on the sidewalk or on ice
snowing softly; *making* a snowman or woman
hiding nuts like a squirrel
striding like a giant taking long, heavy steps
throwing a ball and catching it; *bouncing* a ball
turning like a slow wheel
twirling like a top
waddling like ducks going to the lake for a swim
walking in the mud; up a hill; fast; slowly
wiggling like a worm

PRELIMINARY EXPERIENCES WITH MOVEMENT AND SPACE

1. Ask the children to experiment and decide how many individuals can stand around a table or the teacher's desk without touching one another, or lie on the floor without touching another pupil.
2. They may do the following:
   * Skip around the room without touching anyone; hop like a frog; move backward; or take giant steps;

   * Find a space of their own and reach out as widely as possible without touching anyone;

   * Make the smallest shape they can with their bodies;

   * Walk around in a circle to get the feeling of "circle";

   * Make string squares, triangles, and rectangles on the floor for children to follow; then walk the shapes without string models;

   * Twist from the waist and move the head in the same direction; in the opposite direction;

   * Find a space, plant the feet firmly and pretend they are planted in the ground. Children can then see how many different ways they can move their bodies;

   * Twirl like a top in one spot slower and slower until they stop;

   * Move the feet slowly, then fast, and then slowly again;

   * Pretend to be a balloon sailing in the sky without bumping anyone;

   * Stand in one spot and see how many ways knees can be moved;

21

- Make two buildings from building blocks and see how many ways they can move between blocks without bumping them;

- Make a maze of chairs and other furniture. Try to move through the maze to a set goal. See if there is more than one route to arrive at the goal.

FINGER PLAYS

Children delight in using fingers or effigies to assume characterizations and as an expression of free activity. A finger play provides first steps of the necessary stages of random manipulation which lead to concrete experiences and an expression of them. They provide a basis for abstract thinking.

When a child projects into a finger or uses the body to act out a situation, he/she takes another step in the process of adjusting to the environment. Finger plays are a first step in playing rhymes, since ego expression causes children to use their fingers and hands more frequently than other parts of the body for investigative purposes. These tactile experiences help them to become aware of themselves as people and to feel a sense of control over their surroundings.

The finger play is a dramatic device which leads young children along many avenues of learning.

Fingers

The first one is little and quite fat.

The second finger points like that.

The third one stands tall like a king.

The fourth one wears a little ring.

The fifth one is so very small,

But it's the proudest of them all!

Finger People

Five finger people, left and right,

Met one another on a Saturday night.

People on the right said, "How do you do?"

People on the left said, "Glad to see you."

They began to yawn, and to nod their heads,

And back they went to their soft, warm beds.

(Hold up one hand, and then the other. Move fingers as characters "talk". Lower fingers, put them behind back on the last two lines. Substitute other days of the week.)

Wiggles

A wiggle wiggle here

A wiggle wiggle there

Wiggle your hands up in the air.

Wiggle your shoulders

Wiggle your hips

Wiggle your knees

And move your lips

Wiggle, wiggle, wiggle,

And wiggle some more;

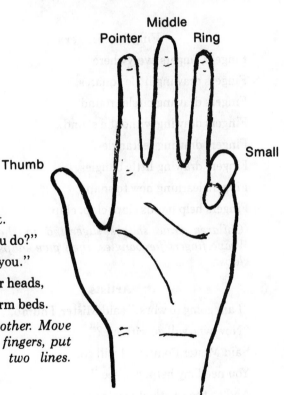

(Children wiggle parts of body.)

And now let's sit down on the floor.

(Move your lips and use no voice. Ask children to watch your face and ask them to wiggle different parts of their bodies.)

A Purse

A purse is a very nice thing to be,

To carry things that are needed for me.

A handkerchief,   (Palms up.)

A penny,   (Make small circle with fingers.)

And one small crayon you see.   (Hold up one finger.)

Fingers, Fingers

Fingers, fingers everywhere

Fingers drawing little squares,

Fingers drawing circles round

Fingers drawing without a sound.

Fingers drawing rectangles,

Fingers drawing little bangles,

Fingers learning how to snap,

Fingers help hands clap, clap, clap!

(Children draw shapes suggested in the air. Weave fingers for bangles, then give snaps and claps.)

Artists

"I am going to work," said Mister Thumb.   (Hold up thumb.)

"Now who will go with me?"

Said Mister Pointer, "I will go.   (Hold up pointer finger.)

You need my help, you see."

And so they worked together,

As happy as could be.

They made a lovely apple

In a big tall apple tree.

They made a little bluebird.

They made a sun for me.

Mister Pointer said, "I like to work."

Mister Thumb said, "I agree."

                                    -Olive Amundson

24

(Ask, "What else can your thumb and pointer finger do? All of your fingers help." Place a few small objects on the floor. Ask one child at a time to use the two fingers and pick them up. A child lays a hand on a piece of paper and another child draws around it. They will have fun drawing around one another's hands and displaying the drawings on a bulletin board.)

Counting Fingers and Toes

I have five fingers.   (Hold up five fingers.)

Look at me.

I have five fingers,

Don't you see   (Count fingers aloud.)

I have five toes   (Hold out foot.)

As everyone knows.

It's fun to have

Five fingers and toes.   (Hold up five fingers and point to toes.)

(Discuss toes of animals. What substitutes do they have for fingers and toes? Penguins - flippers; horses - hooves; birds - wings.)

Fingers in a Row

One, two, three, four, five in a row,

Are fingers on the right, you know.

One, two, three, four, five in a row

Are fingers on the left, and so

How many fingers can you show?

Touch each finger! Ready, go!

One, two, three, four, five,

Six, seven, eight, nine, ten.

That's the way everyone knows -

Ten little fingers in two even rows.

(Before acting out the finger play, be sure that the children know left from right. They count with you and point to each finger. At the end, they bend down each of ten fingers.)

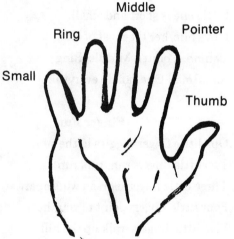

Naming Fingers

Mr. Thumb is strong and small.

Pointer shows the way.

Middle Man stands over all,

Ring Man will obey.

Small man is the tiny one.

I think he has a lot more fun!

(The children point to each finger starting with the thumb.)

Fingers Everywhere

Fingers, fingers here and there.

Fingers wiggling, I declare!   (Wiggle all ten fingers.)

Fingers standing tall and grand.   (Hold fingers erect.)

Fingers bending on each hand.   (Bend down fingers on each hand.)

Fingers, more than just a few.

How many fingers belong to you?   (Children hold up ten fingers.)

(Ask the children to show a few fingers. Show many. Show a few crayons. Show many.)

Describing Fingers

Mister Thumb is short and fat.   (Hold up thumb.)

Maybe he should wear a hat.

Pointer stands up straight, you know.   (Hold up pointer finger.)

He points the way to come and go.

Middle One is strong and tall,   (Hold up middle finger.)

He/she is the longest of them all.

Beside the middle one is Ring.   (Hold up ring finger.)

About our fingers we can sing.

Little one is short and small.   (Hold up little finger.)

I love him/her the most of all.

Thumb, Pointer, Middle, Ring.

And Small One can do everything!

Finger Fun

One little finger wiggles in the sun.

Two little fingers run, run, run!

Three little fingers spread wide apart.

Four little fingers point to your heart.

Five little fingers walk up the hill.

Six little fingers stand straight and still

Seven little fingers climb up a tree.

Eight little fingers fly like a bee.

Nine little fingers scratch in the sand.

All little fingers hide in my hand.   (Make fist.)

(Children follow actions of the rhyme. Encourage them to say the rhyme with you. Ask "What can your fingers do? I will write what you say.")

ABC Fingers

I can make letters with my fingers.

Shall I show you how?

Watch me make the alphabet.

I will do it now.

First, I will make a little *a*.

(Circle with thumb and forefinger, right hand. Use half of pointer finger on other hand for stick.)

Is little *a* your name?

(Response.)

Next, I'll make the better *b*

(Circle with thumb and forefinger on right hand. Use pointer finger on left hand for stick.)

In this finger game.

C is the easiest one to do.

(Curve pointer finger and thumb.)

I will make it now for you.

(Encourage the children to use their fingers to demonstrate other alphabet letters. The d is made opposite to b.)

One Finger, Two

One finger, two fingers,

Belong just to me.

(Pop up small and ring fingers.)

Up pops a third one,

Now there are three.

(Pop up middle finger.)

Up pops a fourth one,

Now there are four.

(Pop up pointer finger.)

Up pops your thumb,

Let's do it once more.

(Pop up thumb.)

(Ordinal and rote counting; watch the coordination as children lift their fingers.)

What Can Your Fingers Do?

What can your fingers do for you?

They can help you tie your shoe.

They can help you button your coat.

They can help you write a note.

They can help you paint and draw.

They can help you hammer and saw.

They can help you put on socks.

They can help you wind up clocks.

They can help you roll up strings.

They can help you pick up things.

They can open; they can close.

They can reach and touch your toes.

Can you think of one or two

Things your fingers do for you?

(Ask, "How do your fingers help you? Show us something you can do with your fingers." Read the poem through once; then read a second time asking children to supply the rhyming words at the end of each line and say the first three words.)

Baby

Baby's fingers,

Baby's nose,

Baby's head,

And baby's toes,

Baby's ears,

Baby's eyes,

Baby's arms,

And baby's thighs.

Baby's neck,

Baby's cheeks,

Baby's shoulders,

Baby peeks.

Baby's mouth,

Baby's hips,

Baby's thumb,

And baby's lips.

(Cover your eyes and say, "Peek-a-Boo".)

(The child may use a doll with limber arms or a puppet. The puppet then points to each part of the body. Ask, "Do you have a baby at home? If you do, learn this rhyme and play it with your baby." Advised for preschool use.)

28

What the Fingers Said

The fingers went to walk one day,

And this is what I heard them say:

Thumb said, "I am so fat, you see,

But no one ever laughs at me."

Pointer said this with a shout:

"Folks need ME to point things out!"

Middle said, "I'm very long,

But I keep the others strong."

Ring said, "Important I must be

When someone puts a ring on me."

Little One said, "Oh, please don't fuss.

_____ needs all of us!"

(Substitute the name of a child each time the rhyme is said. The children point to one finger at a time.)

Fingers and Toes

I have ten fingers;	(Hold up fingers.)
I have ten toes.	(Point to feet.)
They help very much as everyone knows.	
I do not wish to have fins like a fish,	(Motion of swimming.)
Or paws like a dog,	(Double up fists.)
Or webs like a frog,	(Spread hands.)
Or claws like a bear,	(Make claws of fingers.)
Or hooves like a mare,	(Double fists.)
Or scales like a snake,	(Wiggle fingers.)
Make no mistake!	
I have ten fingers,	(Repeat motions.)
I have ten toes.	
They help very much as everyone knows!	
My fingers feel	
They can turn a wheel.	(Turn hand around.)
They can hold a cat,	(Cradle arms.)
Hit a ball with a bat.	(Hold imaginary bat with two hands.)
My toes like the sand,	
And they help me to stand.	
My toes can tiptoe,	

And wade in the snow.

I have ten fingers,

I have ten toes.

They help very much as everyone knows!

(Tell what else your ten fingers and ten toes can do.)

My Hand

My hand scoops things up.   (Cup hand.)

It holds things like a cup.

It can make a tight fist,   (Make fist.)

Hold a grocery list,   (Pretend to hold a paper slip.)

Or spread out flat,   (Spread hand, palm down.)

Give a friendly pat.   (Pat someone on hand.)

It can sift dirt and sand.   (Spread fingers.)

My hand really is grand—

My fine five-fingered hand.

(Ask: "How does your hand help you here at school? Do you use your right or left hand when you paint? Do people use only one hand when they play the piano? type? Pretend to hold a crayon and write your name in the air.")

(Repeat motions.)

ACTION RHYMES

"What children imitate, they begin to understand. Let them represent the flying of birds and they will enter partially into the life of birds. Let them imitate the rapid motion of fishes in the water, and their sympathy with fishes is quickened. Let them reproduce the activities of a farmer or baker, and their eyes are opened to the meaning of work. In one word, let them reflect in their play the varied aspects of life, and their thoughts will begin to grapple with significance."
-Friederich Froebel

Matching

Match the fingers on your hands.

One to one as up they stand.

Match your two thumbs small and fat.

Match two pointers just like that.

Match two middle fingers tall.

Match two ring ones. That's not all.

Match two fingers very small.

Match two feet with socks and shoes.

Match everything that goes by two's.

(Hold up fingers on both hands as they are mentioned. Ask, "What else can we match? two shoulders? two arms? legs? lips? cheeks? ears? eyes? sleeves? buttons? pencils? erasers?")

Walking

Walk very slowly,	(Children follow directions.)
Hands by your sides.	
Walk to the corner,	
And now please hide.	(Hands over faces.)
Walk very quickly.	(Walk rapidly.)
But do not run.	
Walk to the corner,	
Face the warm sun.	(Circle with arms.)
Walk on your tiptoes,	(Walk on tiptoes.)
Now on your heels.	(Walk on heels.)
Make both your arms	
Go around like wheels.	(Both arms move in a circle.)
Walk to the chalkboard.	(Walk slowly.)
Walk like a clown.	(Strut or waddle.)
Walk like a turtle,	(Creep.)
Sit quietly down.	

(This rhyme can also be used for relaxation as well as for varied movements.)

31

Small and Tall

Make yourself as tall as a house.	(Stand erect.)
Make yourself small as a little mouse.	(Curl up on floor.)
Shake your finger.	(Move pointer finger.)
Tap your feet.	(Tap three times.)
Now close your eyes,	
And go to sleep.	(Children relax with eyes closed.)

(This rhyme can also be used for relaxation.)

Stand Tall

Stand up tall
Like a wall.
Take two steps backward;
Do not fall.
Raise your hands
Away up high.
Lower your hands,
And make a sigh.
Keep your feet
In one place.
Twist your hips,
And touch your face.
Sit down quietly,
You are through.
Now you know
What you can do!

(Children stand and perform all of the movements suggested in the rhyme.)

Heels and Toes

Heels and toes,
Heels and toes.
We can do things
With heels and toes.
Up, up, up,
One, two, three.
Can you stand
Tiptoe for me?
Down, down, down,
On your heels.
Can you tell me
How that feels?
Down on heels,
Up on toes,
Everyone knows
About heels and toes.

(Ask volunteers to take off their shoes for this action game. They follow movements suggested.)

There Were Ten in a Bed

There were ten in a bed,
And one of them said,
"Roll over, roll over,"
And they all rolled over,
And one fell out!
There were nine in a bed,
And one of them said,
"Roll over, roll over,"
And they all rolled over,
And one fell out!
There were eight in a bed,
And one of them said,
"Roll over, roll over,"
And they all rolled over,
And one fell out!
End the poem in this way:
There was none in the bed,
And nobody said,
"Roll over, roll over."
So no one rolled over,
And no one fell out.

-An old English Rhyme

(The children lie in a row on the rug. Each one rolls over once, then one at a time leaves the rug. A child may tap a triangle when one falls out of the bed.)

Me

Here are my fingers and here is my nose.
Here are my ears, and here are my toes.
Here are my eyes that are open and wide.
Here is my mouth with my white teeth inside.
Here is my pink tongue that helps me to speak.
Here are my shoulders and here is each cheek.
Here are my hands that will help me play.
Here are my feet that go walking each day.

(Children point to each part of the body as it is mentioned. This is a drill on verbals: "Here is" and "Here are.")

Following Directions

Please stand on tiptoes.   (Teacher.)
I will stand on tiptoes.   (Children.)
Wiggle your nose.
I will wiggle my nose.
Please reach up high.
I will reach up high.
Point to the sky.
I will point to the sky.
Wave your right hand.
I will wave my right hand.
Stand and look grand.
I will stand and look grand.
Please jump in one place.
I will jump in one place.
Please cover your face.
I will cover my face.

(Once the children grow accustomed to the rhyme, suggest that volunteers take turns at giving directions. After several participations, you may want to change "I will" to "I'll" since children with substandard speech often have a problem with words that are contracted.)

Jumping Jack

I am a little jumping jack.
I jump out of my box and I jump right back.
I jump up high, I bend down low
For that is the way that I must go.
I jump to the left, I jump to the right,
I jump in my box and I hide out of sight.
I jump up and down and I turn all around,
And I jump right out and land on the ground.

(Secure a large empty box that will hold a child comfortably. The children say the rhyme with you and take turns at being the jumping jack.)

Reaching and Clapping

Reach with both hands toward the ceiling,

Reach with both hands toward the floor,

Reach with left hand toward the left wall,

Reach with right hand toward the door.

Clap three times; face the ceiling.

Clap three times; face the floor,

Clap three times; face the left wall,

Clap three times; face the door.

Will you point at the window?   (Soft voice.)

Will you point at the door?

Will you point at me and say, "Hi!"

Will you sit down on the floor?

(Say the rhyme slowly and stop at the end of each motion. The second time use no voice. Ask the children to watch your face and mouth and follow your silent words. Use as readiness to precede a learning activity.)

I Can Raise My Right Hand

I can raise my right hand.

   I can raise it high.

I can wave my right hand

   At an airplane in the sky.

I can raise my left hand.

   I can raise it high.

I can wave my left hand

   At an airplane in the sky.

(The children perform all actions. Before beginning the poem, ask them to demonstrate the left and right hands.)

Little and Big Me

I'm a great, tall pine tree

Standing on a hill.

I'm a little bitty blade of grass

Sitting very still.

I'm a tiny, teeny, weeny

Little, bitty elf.

I'm a great big giant,

So proud of myself.

(Children act out the rhyme. Say, "Show us how you would be a tall tree; a tiny blade of grass. Make yourself into a little elf. Now make yourself into a huge giant.")

Shapes

Here is a big, round doughnut.

Here is a little, round hole.

Here is a short little blade of grass.

Here's a tall, tall telephone pole.

(Make large circle with fingers and thumbs.)

(Make small circle with fingers.)

(Crouch down.)

(Reach arms high and stand on tiptoe.)

Who Feels Happy Today?

Who feels happy at school today?

All who do, snap your fingers this way.

Who feels happy at school today?

All who do, clap your hands this way.

Who feels happy at school today?

All who do, wink your eye this way.

Who feels happy at school today?

All who do, fold your hands this way.

(Ask, "What makes you feel happy? Can we think of other things to do with our bodies when we are happy? Show us a motion that you like to do.")

Active You

You wiggle your thumbs and clap your hands,

And then you stamp your feet.

You turn to the left, you turn to the right

And make your fingers meet.

You raise them high and let them down;

You give another clap.

You wave your hands and fold your hands,

And put them in your lap.

(Follow directions for movements stated in the rhyme. Say the rhyme very slowly at first, since some children's coordination will not permit quick movements. Use for readiness.)

What I Can Do

I can spin just like a top.

Look at me! Look at me!

I have feet and I can hop.

Look at me! Look at me!

I have hands and I can clap.

Look at me! Look at me!

I can lay them in my lap.

Look at me! Look at me!

(The children act out this rhyme. Ask, "What else can your feet do? What else can your hands do?" Encourage individuals to make up their own rhymes about their accomplishments with hands and feet. Write down their words and make a booklet of them.)

Licks

Here is a round, sweet lollipop.

I bought it today at a candy shop.

One lick, mmm, it tastes so good.

Two licks, oh, I knew it would.

Three licks, yes, I like the taste.

Four licks, now I will not waste.

Five licks, keep on and on.

Six licks, oh! It's nearly gone!

Seven licks, it's getting small.

Eight licks, and still not all.

Nine licks, my tongue goes fast.

Ten licks, and that's the last!

(The child traces around circles to make lollipops from construction paper. Cover with acetate. Attach to a dowel stick. Choose ten children at a time to act out the rhyme. Warn them not to really lick the paper, but just pretend.)

Hold Your Head High

Hold your head high,

With hands in the air.

Now let's sit down,

Each in a chair.

Let's clap three times,

Then make a frown.

Let's laugh, "Ha, ha!"

And flop right down.

(Children follow directions in the rhyme. Ask, "Can you flop down like an empty sack and make no noise at all?")

Tippy, Tippy Tiptoe

Tippy, tippy tiptoe,

There they go;

Ten little hungry mice

Walking in a row.   (Move fingers of both hands to right.)

They couldn't find a thing to eat,

And so they had to go

Tippy, tippy tiptoe,   (Move ten fingers to the left.)

Tippy, tippy tiptoe,

Tippy, tippy tiptoe...   (Continue until voice fades to a whisper.)

         -Adapted from an old English rhyme

Finger Taps

Barbara taps with one finger tap; tap.

Barbara taps with one finger tap; tap.

Barbara taps with one finger tap; tap.

On this special day.

Billy taps with two finger taps; tap, tap.

Billy taps with two finger taps; tap, tap.

Billy taps with two finger taps; tap, tap.

On this special day.

(Continue the rhyme by using names of various children in the group. After the number five is reached, start with a different group. The class will say the word tap *whenever it occurs. End the rhyme in this way: "Everyone goes to rest now. Close eyes." [Say three times] "On this special day.")*

Parts of the Body

Head and shoulders, knees and toes,
   knees and toes;

Head and shoulders, knees and toes,
   knees and toes.

Eyes and ears and mouth and nose,
   mouth and nose;

Eyes and ears and mouth and nose,
   mouth and nose.

AND THAT'S THE WAY
   THIS RHYME GAME GOES!

(Children stand and touch each part of the body as it is mentioned with their hands. One child lies on a large piece of wrapping paper while another traces the body outline. Reverse the procedure until all children are traced. Each child inserts features and cuts out his/her own shape. Ask, "Does this paper model take up more space than you, yourself?")

Indicating Body Parts

Touch your left knee, then your right;

Touch your left thumb of small height.

Raise your right hand to the sky;

With your right hand, touch your eye.

Now, please shake hands with a friend;

Touch your left foot down at the end.

Touch your left ear, then your shoulder;

Show me left before you're older!

Touch your right leg, and left hip;

Touch your upper and lower lip.

(Say the rhyme very slowly so that children will have ample time to think in terms of "left" and "right." If movements are too fast, children will have difficulty in following directions.)

Open Your Fingers

Open your fingers.	(Show ten fingers.)
Make a fist tight.	(Fist.)
Now put your hands	
Away out of sight.	(Hands behind back.)
Show us two hands.	(Hold up both hands.)
Now let them clap.	(Clap twice.)
Now lay them quietly	
Inside your lap.	(Fold hands in lap.)
Reach your ten fingers	
High, high, high!	(Lift arms.)
Pretend you're a robin in the sky!	(Motion of flying.)

If You Can

If you can stand on the tip of your toes,	(Children act out.)
I will give you a red, red rose.	(Hold up one finger.)
If you can stand away back on your heels,	(Children act out.)
I will give you two orange peels.	(Hold up two fingers.)
If you can bend down and touch the floor,	(Children act out.)
I will give you three apple cores.	(Hold up three fingers.)
If you can twist to the left and the right,	(Children act out.)
I will give you four candy bites.	(Hold up four fingers.)
If you can reach your hands to the sky,	(Children act out.)
I will give you five pieces of pie	(Hold up five fingers.)
I wish that this game were not pretend,	
And I am sorry that it has to end.	

(Ask, "Would you like this game to go on? What are other things you can do with your fingers, hands, and body?" Below are other rhymes that might be added.)

If you can stamp and give six kicks,
I will give you six lollipop licks.
If you can stand and stretch up tall,
I will give you seven popcorn balls.
If you can blink and nod your head,
I will give you eight slices of bread.
If you can jump high up in the air,
I will give you nine juicy pears.
If you can stand and bend your knees,
I will give you ten slices of cheese.

Size, Space, and Time
(A Concept Rhyme)

Mr. Large and Mr. Small.	(Make large circle, then a small one.)
Mr. Short and Mr. Tall.	(Lower self and then stand tall.)
Mr. Thin and Mr. Fat.	(Measure sizes with hands.)
Mr. Curved and Mr. Flat.	(Wave hand for curved and hold out palm for flat.)
Mr. Left and Mr. Right.	(Show each hand.)
Mr. Heavy and Mr. Light	(Point to the desk and then to piece of cotton.)
Mr. High and Mr. Low	(Point up high and then to floor.)
Mr. Fast and Mr. Slow	(Take fast steps in place, then slow ones.)
Mr. Round and Mr. Square.	(Draw figures in air.)
Mr. Here and Mr. There.	(Point to neighbor, then out the window.)
Mr. Far and Mr. Near.	(Point out window, then to rug.)
Mr. Month and Mr. Year.	(Point to calendar.)
Mr. Crooked and Mr. Straight.	(Makes lines with hands.)
Mr. Early and Mr. Late.	(Point to clock.)
Mr. Walk and Mr. Run.	(Walk in place, then run in place.)
Mr. Some and Mr. None.	(Show five fingers, then hide in fist.)

(Discuss all of the concepts before reading the rhyme. Encourage the children to say the rhyme with you even on a first reading. Use pantomime to make the words more graphic. Discuss the calendar: show the days, show the months, and show one year. Discuss concepts early *and* late. *Say, "If you were to come to school at noon, you would be late. If you came before the sun rose, you would be early." Call attention to objects in the room that are* large *and* small, *and make drawings on the board to illustrate* crooked, straight, *and so on. Think of other concepts that can be presented, such as* above *and* below, *empty* and *full. You may wish to change some of the designations to* Mrs. *and* Ms.)

Here is Our World

Here is our world, our big, round world.   (Spread arms.)

Here are the mountains high.   (Stretch arms up.)

Here is a fish that swims in the sea.   (Move hand back and forth.)

Here are the birds that fly.   (Motion of flying.)

Here is the sun, the bright, warm sun.   (Make circle of arms.)

Here are the leaves that fall.   (Let raised hands fall gently.)

Here is our world, our big, round world,
And God has made it all.   (Spread arms.)

-Traditional

Playing a Drum

Tumpity, tumpity, tum.

_____ is playing a drum.

One little girl/boy is dancing around.

When she/he hears that tumpity, tumpity
sound.

Tumpity, tumpity, tum.

_____ is playing a drum.

One little boy/girl is hopping around

When he/she hears that tumpity, tumpity
sound.

-Traditional

(Substitute names of children each time. Use a real drum and let children take turns playing it softly with fingers for the various actions. These additional actions may be used: jumping, skipping, walking, leaping, tiptoeing, running. Individuals volunteer as participants.)

Things to Do

Tap your head and tap your toes.

Curl yourself up like a garden hose.

Stretch yourself long; make yourself wide,

Stand up tall with your hands by your side.

(Ask, "Show how you would curl up like a garden hose. Could you do all of these things?")

I'm a Limp Rag Doll

I'm a limp rag doll with no bones at all.

I flip and I flop when I try to stand tall.

I flip and I flop when I try to sit down.

Some people think that I act like a clown.

I flip and I flop and I flop some more.

I guess I will just have to flop on the floor.

I am tired of flipping and flopping this way;

So I think I will just have to stop for today.

(Children move to right and left on the words flip and flop. Try to bring in a Raggedy Ann or Andy doll to demonstrate the motions. Other motions: "Bow from the waist for the clown." "Stretch out on the floor" at the end of the rhyme.)

During the Week

On Monday, I will jump up high,	(Children jump up and down.)
And stretch until I reach the sky.	(Reach upward.)
On Tuesday, I will bend down low,	(Children bend from knees.)
And like a flower, slowly grow.	(Crouch and then slowly rise.)
On Wednesday, I will stand up tall,	(Children stand tall.)
And march and march around the hall.	(Take marching steps in one place.)
On Thursday, I will turn around,	(Turn.)
And slowly sink down to the ground.	(Sink to floor gradually.)
On Friday, I will bend my knees,	(Bend knees.)
And gallop off among the trees.	(Gallop in one place.)
On Saturday, I will hop and hop,	(Hop in one place.)
Then spin around just like a top.	(Turn around several times.)
On Sunday, I will nod my head,	(Nod head.)
And tiptoe quietly to bed.	(Tiptoe to seat.)

(Use with Favorite Nursery Songs, *Phyllis Brown Ohanian; Random House, New York, 1956.)*

Making a Puppet Talk

Puppet (or name), sit down in a chair.	(Bend one hand down to form a seat for a chair. Place the back of the other hand inside the hand puppet.)
Clap your hands, and touch your hair	(Clap; then reach one finger to stroke hair.)
Wave your hand and raise it high.	(Wave puppet's hand; then point arm up.)
Put it down and touch one eye.	(Raise arm to touch puppet's eye.)
Jump up and down, and bow your head.	(Make movements.)
Turn right around and jump into bed.	(Turn whole body of puppet; then take off puppet and lay it on the table.)

(Encourage hand puppet talk. The child asks a question and the puppet answers in another voice. Questions and answers can reveal much about the child and the family. A silent child often can let a puppet express itself. Allow a child to stand behind an easel and hold up a hand puppet.)

I Am a Sunflower

I am a sunflower

Growing by the hour. (Children move slowly upward.)

Now I am grown,

And my petals full-blown. (Children stand tall.)

I turn to the right, (Turn head to right.)

And I face the light. (Make circle for sun.)

The sun sets in the West, (Turn head to left.)

And I have my rest. (Clasped hands beside face.)

I awake with the sun, (Make circle for sun.)

A new day has begun.

(Show a picture of a sunflower. Ask, "Why do you think it is called a sunflower?")

Hands on Shoulders

Hands on shoulders; hands on knees;

Hands behind you, if you please!

Touch your hips and touch your nose.

Bend way down and touch your toes.

Hands up high, now, in the air;

Down at sides, and touch your hair.

Hands up high as you did before.

Clap your hands: one, two, three, four!

(A long mirror may be provided so that the children can take turns watching their motions as they say the rhyme. Trace flat hand prints on red and green construction paper, red for left and green for right. Provide an association with traffic lights. Mount hand prints on white construction paper, label them, and tack them on the bulletin board.)

Honey Bear

Honey Bear, sit in a chair,

Clap your hands,

And comb your hair.

Wave one hand;

Point toward town.

Touch your knees,

And jump up and down.

Raise your arms,

Bow your head;

Turn around twice,

And jump into bed.

(Suggest that the children act out this rhyme in their own way, creating their own actions. Say, "Pretend that you are teddy bears." If a hand "bear" puppet is available, invite individuals to let it perform the actions.)

Opposites

Right hand, left hand,	(Show right, then left hand.)
Up and down,	(Point up, then down.)
Over and under,	(Hand makes jumping motion, then scoops.)
Smile and frown,	(Smile, then frown.)
Sad and glad,	(Look sad, then happy.)
Wake and sleep,	(Open eyes, then close them.)
Large and small,	(Measure.)
Give and keep,	(Hold out palm, then hide it behind back.)
Long and short,	(Measure.)
High and low,	(Point high, then to floor.)
Loud and soft,	(Voice is loud on the word loud; whisper the word soft.)
Come and go,	(Beckon with finger, then make shoving motion.)
Here and there,	(Point to floor, and then window.)
He and she,	(Point to a boy, then a girl.)
One and none,	(Hold up one finger, then form zero with forefinger and thumb.)
You and me!	(Point to other person and then self.)

Pendulum

The clock ticks,	(Pointer finger moves back and forth.)
The clock tocks.	
Left and right,	
Left and right,	
And never stops.	
Tick, tock! Tick, tock!	(Voice fades as tick-tock is repeated.)

Tip-Toe

Tip-toe, tip-toe	(Children tip-toe.)
That is how the pixies go.	
Tip-toe, tip-toe,	
They can hear the flowers grow.	(Cup ear with hand.)
Tip-toe, tip-toe,	
Silently they come and go.	
Tip-toe, tip-toe,	
Quiet as white flakes of snow.	(Raise arms and lower them, moving fingers.)
Tip-toe, tip-toe,	
Tip-toe, tip-toe.	(Repeat until voice fades to a whisper.)

(Say: "Show how you would tip-toe like a pixie." Children may tiptoe around the room and as they whisper, return to their seats.)

42

Hands on Hips

Hands on hips; now turn around.

Plant your feet here in the ground.

Twist your hips, now stretch and bend.

Turn around. Smile at a friend.

Bend your body; sway and sway,

That is all we'll do today!

(Read very slowly so that the children will have sufficient time to perform each action. Use for readiness.)

I Can Do Lots of Things

I can be an airplane flying in the air. (Hold out arms and let body sway.)

I can have four feet and walk just like a bear. (Bend over and take awkward steps.)

I can be a monkey climbing up a tree. (Motion of climbing.)

I can be a buzzing yellow bumblebee. (Twirl forefinger and buzz.)

I can be a pony galloping around. (Make three galloping steps.)

I can be a little mole hiding in the ground. (Hug body and close eyes.)

I can be a frog puffing out his chest. (Puff out chest.)

I can be a bird sitting on a nest. (Sit on floor.)

I can be a porcupine with needles on my back. (Spread ten fingers.)

I can be a yellow duck: quack, quack, quack. (Put pointer finger and thumb together; move them.)

I can be a fish swimming in the sea. (Wavy motion with hand.)

I can be just anything that I want to be!

(Say the rhyme slowly so that children will have time to perform the actions. Before saying it, ask individuals to tell how they would gallop, walk like a bear, and so on.)

Twelve Months

January brings the snow.

Cold wind makes our faces glow. (Hug body.)

February brings valentines (Draw heart shape in air.)

With written messages on lines.

March brings winds to fly a kite. (Wave hand back and forth.)

Up among the clouds of white.

April brings the pattering rain (Hands held high; moving fingers lowered.)

So that seeds will grow again.

May is time to dance and sing (Take dance steps.)

We are so glad that it is spring.

June brings flowers dainty sweet.   (Hold out hand.)

Skates go skimming down the street.   (Slide feet along floor.)

July, the Fourth we celebrate,

A very patriotic date.   (Pretend to wave flag.)

August days we ride around,

On the merry, merry, merry-go-round.   (Whirl hand around and around.)

September, school begins and then

We can see our friends again.   (Shake hands with person next to you.)

October brings us Halloween

When many ghostly sights are seen.   (Encircle eyes with fingers.)

November days bring cloudy skies,

Cranberry sauce, and pumpkin pies.   (Make circle with fingers.)

December brings the Christmas tree   (Point fingers to represent tree.)

And (Santa Claus) for you and me.   (Point to someone and then self.)
    (Hanukkah)

(Turn the calendar to each of these months. Ask, "Which month do you like best? Why? Which ones are school months? Vacation months? Show us on the calendar. Why do we need calendars? Which one is an exciting month?")

Small and Round

Small and round, small and round.   (Make circle with thumb and pointer finger.)

A bulb is deep inside the ground.   (Crouch to floor.)

Stretch and grow, stretch and grow;

Up the stalk comes, slowly—slow.   (Rise slowly.)

Buds are seen, buds are seen.   (Show fists.)

The petals grow and they are green.   (Release one finger at a time.)

Straight and tall, straight and tall   (Raise fingers high.)

Flowers grow beside the wall.   (Lower fingers and cup palms.)

Hawaiian Rain

The sun is gone.   (Hold hands above head and outline circle with fingers.)

The wind is free.   (Extend one arm. Make circle over head with the other.)

The sea is angry   (Beat hands in the air left and right, right and left.)

As can be.

Here comes a shower   (Bring hands down and wiggle fingers.)

Out of the sky;

And a rainbow will follow   (Use arms to show arc of a rainbow.)

By and by.

44

I Love the Hills

I love the hills,

(Cross arms across chest and turn head to one side. Lift hands over head. Bring one hand up to represent peak of a hill.)

And the stars at night.

(Cross index and middle fingers on each hand.)

I love the moon

(Cross arms over chest and turn face to one side. Hold hands above head and outline circle for moon.

And the day so bright.

I love the tradewinds.

(Repeat action of *love*. Extend one arm. Circle over head with other arm.)

They sing to me

(Bring both hands to mouth.)

Of happy times,

(Fingertips together and elbows to side; sway.)

And ships at sea.

(Beat hands in air, left to right, right to left.)

(Use Learn to Dance the Hula *by Eileen O'Brien; Tong Publishing Company, Honolulu, 1958.)*

QUIET TIMES

All children need rest and feelings of serenity at times during the day to satisfy their growing needs. Security lies in order and some routine. Therefore, all children require a well-planned program so that disorganization can be prevented.

Relaxation occurs when pressures are removed so that ideas can flow freely. Although work can be relaxing, it is important for a child to experience some planned relaxation periods through use of the rhymes and ideas which follow.

Baby Birds

We are baby robins in a nest.

We are yawning . . . nodding . . . stretching.   (Children act out.)

We have all been fed,

And now we're in bed.

We are yawning . . . nodding . . . stretching.

-Traditional

My Hinges

My neck has hinges that move it so.   (Move neck to left and right.)

My shoulders have hinges, just see them go.   (Move shoulders up and down.)

My hands and my arms have hinges, too.   (Move arms and fingers.)

My waist will show what hinges can do.   (Move left to right at waist.)

It bends to the front; it bends to the back.   (Bend back and bend forward.)

I hope that my hinges never will crack!

My knees have hinges, just see them bend.

My legs have hinges down to the end.

My body has hinges. They do not break.

I use every hinge when I am awake.

(Ask: "What do we mean by hinges?" Point to the door. "The door has hinges that help open and shut it. What happens to hinges on a door when they are never used? They rust. Maybe they squeak. If we do not keep our bodies exercised, the joints (hinges) might not work properly. Show us how we would walk if we had no joints in our bodies. How would we look? Can you name some of the places in this room we might find hinges? A box? What else? Let's do the rhyme again. Then we can wake up all of the hinges in our bodies.")

46

Yawns

I saw a puppy yawn and yawn—ow—ooop!

I caught the yawns and then

I yawned—and yawned—and yawned—Ho hum!   (Children yawn.)

And then I yawned again.

I saw my kitten yawning.

I had to stop my play.

I yawned at least one minute,

And yawned the yawns away.

The animals make me sleepy,

With mouths so yawning wide.

I must relax and close my eyes.

I feel so many yawns inside.

(Bring in a picture of a person or animal yawning. Watch to see if anyone "catches" the yawn. Yawn widely to see if anyone can "catch" your yawn. Ask, "Have you seen your pet yawn? Show how it is done. Make a sound that goes with the yawn." Read The Sleepy Little Lion *by Margaret Wise Brown; Harper and Row, New York, 1947.)*

I Am a Little Puppet Clown

I am a funny puppet clown;

Loosen my strings and my head will fall down.   (Flop head.)

First I will stand; then I'll fall down.   (Act out.)

I am a funny puppet clown.

I am a funny puppet man.

The people call me Puppet Dan.

Hold me up so I will not fall.   (Stand tall.)

Let go my string, and I'll surely fall.   (Sink to floor.)

(Bring in a puppet which is manipulated by strings and let it go through the motions of the clown.)

Stretch, Stretch

Stretch, stretch away up high.   (Reach arms upward.)

Stretch and try to reach the sky.   (Stand on tiptoes and reach.)

Be a bird, fly to a tree.   (Motion of flying.)

Be a fish, swim in the sea.   (Swim.)

Sway and sway just like a breeze   (Sway back and forth, with hip action.)

Now pretend you're going to sneeze!

Floppy Clown

I am a great big floppy clown.   (Flop.)

I bend away back; I bend away down.   (Bend body back and forth.)

I smile a big smile; and then I frown.   (Smile and frown.)

I am a great big floppy clown.   (Flop.)

I'm tired of flopping, so when I sleep   (Hands folded beside face.)

I'll fall down in a great big heap.   (Fall gently without making a sound.)

Counting for Rest Time

Go to rest while I count one: One.   (Children may count with you softly.)

Now our resting time's begun.

Go to rest while I count two: One, two.

Let this music play for you.   (Use music box.)

Go to rest while I count three: One, two, three.

Think some quiet thoughts with me.

Go to rest while I count four: One, two, three, four.

Sit relaxed upon the floor.

Go to rest while I count five: One, two, three, four, five.

Breathe softly. We are so alive.

Now, let's count from one to ten: (Children count aloud in soft voices.)

One, two, three, four, five, six, seven, eight, nine, ten.

Now, you are all awake! What would you like to make?

48

(You may substitute an activity such as "Now you may all write again. Now you can go play again. Now you can go back to your work again.")

Sleepy Kitten

A kitten stretches.   (Children stretch.)

And makes herself long.   (Stretch again.)

Then she hums a soft

Little purring song.   (Children whisper the word *purr* several times.)

She yawns a big yawn.   (Children yawn.)

She stretches some more.   (Children stretch again.)

And then she falls fast asleep on the floor. (Place palms together beside head.)

Progressive Relaxation

Quiet Time

Your feet are quiet—they feel still.

Your legs are quiet—your body is quiet.

Your fingers are not moving.

Your hands are not moving.

Your arms are not moving.

Your shoulders are still, your neck is still.

Your face is still—your eyes are closed.

It feels good to be quiet inside.

Now you may wake up slowly... slowly ... slowly...

You can feel still.

I knew you could.

You could feel still.

Didn't it feel good?

(This is a projected type of relaxation where children follow directions and gain a feeling of repose. Read It's Time to Go to Bed *by Joyce Segal; Doubleday, Garden City, New York, 1979.)*

Be quiet, feet,

Be quiet, legs,

Be a hen sitting on eggs.

Be quiet, fingers.

Be quiet, wrists,

Let your hands make tiny fists.

Be quiet, shoulders,

Be quiet, chest.

Be a bird asleep in a nest.

(Ask, "What other parts of the body can you ask to be quiet? Why would a hen have to be quiet sitting on eggs? Show how a bird would sleep in a nest.")

Make Yourself Tall

Make yourself tall

Raise your hands in the air.

Please sit down

In your very own chair.

Clap three times

Make a great big frown.

Laugh, "Ha, ha!"

And flop like a clown.

(Resting Time Music: "Quiettime" from We All Live Together, *Vol. 1, Young Heart Music Education Service; Beethoven's Symphony No. 6, "The Pastoral Symphony.")*

Relaxing Flowers

Five pretty sunflowers	(Hold up five fingers.)
Are standing in the sun;	
Now their heads are nodding,	(Bend fingers lightly.)
And bowing one by one.	(Move fingers back and forth.)
Down, down, down, down	
Comes the gentle rain	(Raise hands, wiggle fingers, and lower arms.)
And the five pretty sunflowers	
Lift up their heads again.	(Hold up five fingers.)

(Use also as a spring poem.)

How They Rest

Pups put heads between their paws.

Kittens curl up in a ball.

Little frogs sit by a pond,

Horses stand in a stall.

Birds hide heads beneath their wings.

Sheep lie down near a shed.

I don't do any of these things at all.

I sleep in my own little bed.

(Read the rhyme slowly and softly. Ask, "How does your pet sleep? Where? What do you like to do before bedtime? Tell how other animals sleep. How do animals in the zoo sleep?")

Growing Up

Up, up, very slowly,	(Move very slowly upward.)
Up, up, I am going.	
Up, up, very slowly,	
Look at me; I am growing.	
Down, down, very slowly,	(Move slowly downward.)
Now I am a mole.	
Down, down very slowly.	
I am in a dark hole.	

(This rhyme demands excellent control of body movement as the child rises and sinks to the floor.)

Tiptoeing

I tiptoe here and I tiptoe there.

I tiptoe as lightly as wings in the air.

I tiptoe along in my two little shoes;

I tiptoe softly as kitten mews.

I tiptoe slowly with no rush.

I tiptoe quietly as a hush.

I tiptoe here and I tiptoe there,

And I tiptoe over to sit in my chair.

(A small group of children tiptoe around the room as they say the rhyme with you. On the last line they sit in their chairs as you choose other children.)

Tiptoeing in the Dark

Upstairs, downstairs,

Quiet as a mouse;

Tiptoe, tiptoe,

All around the house.

Tiptoe, tiptoe,

Creep and creep about;

I hope the wind won't come along

And blow my candle out!

-Adapted from an unknown author

(Children tiptoe up and down a set of stairs, if one is available, or around in a large circle. They may carry a make-believe candle or a real one.)

Nap Time

One little puppy jumps on my lap.

He takes a nap in Daddy's cap.

One little kitten purrs a tune.

She takes a nap every afternoon.

One little boy/girl with curly head

Knows it is time to go to bed.

(Children close their eyes as they listen to you read the rhyme. Ask, "How does this rhyme about naps make you feel?")

A Quiet Time

The sun has gone down

Over the town.

Sh.... sh.... sh....!

Make believe it is night;

And there is no light.

Sh.... sh.... sh....!

Each eye must close,

And now you can doze.

Sh.... sh.... sh....!

Count slowly to nine:

1,2,3,4,5,6,7,8,9.

Then, wake up and shine!

COUNTING

Counting holds great satisfaction for young children. Even though they may not understand the significance of the concept of five or ten as they recite a finger play or an action rhyme, rote counting should not be minimized. Rhymes not only familiarize the children with numbers and number names as well as numerical order, but also aid them in developing the meaning of "more than," "one more than," or "less than" ideas of counting. Through the addition and subtraction concepts in rhyme, repetition and imagery contained in this book, children are led into meaningful counting; for example, when the child is observing five fingers and does not need to count them, but can see five at a glance, and can determine number property.

When saying these counting rhymes, the children also begin to associate ordinals (first, second, third) with one, two, and three, and consequently with numerals 1, 2, and 3.

$1\ 2\ 3\ 4\ 5$

Fun with Numbers

Five little pigs were eating corn. (Five together.)

Two little pigs went to the barn. (Two leave.)

Two more left and went to the pen. (Two leave.)

One more left—I don't know when. (One leaves.)

Two and two and one said, "We'd rather

We five pigs all got back together." (Five return.)

(Acting out these simple rhymes will give the children an idea of number concepts, such as taking away and sets.)

Six Little Bunnies

Six little bunnies liked to play. (Six children.)

Two little bunnies hopped away. (Two leave.)

And that left _____ bunnies to run and play. (Children substitute number.)

Two little bunnies began to race. (Two leave.)

And that left _____ to run and play.

Two little bunnies deserted the place. (Two leave.)

And that left _____ bunnies to run and race.

But before you could say, "Tick-tick-tack,"

Six of the bunnies came running back. (Six return.)

(Provide a rug or a special area for the set. The selection provides practice for subtracting by two's. Count with the children: Two, four, six, eight, ten, as they show fingers adding two more. Explain the term deserted-went away or left. Explain two meanings of left-direction and leaving. Listen for the "z" sound at the end of the word bunnies. Ask the class to say with you: "One bunny, two bunnies.")

Five Little Puppies

Five little puppies gnawed on a bone.

One little puppy left her home.   (One leaves.)

One little puppy went to eat.   (One leaves.)

One little puppy ran down the street.   (One leaves.)

Two little puppies were scared by a frog.   (Two leave.)

But all five went home to their Mother Dog.   (Five return.)

(Five children sit on the floor and one at a time leaves. All return.)

Five Little Mice

Five little mice went out to play.

One little mouse scampered far away.

So _____ little mice were left to play.

One little mouse thought she wouldn't stay,

So _____ little mice were left to play.

One little mouse saw cheese on a tray,

So _____ little mice were left to play.

One little mouse took a holiday,

So _____ little mouse was left to play.

One little mouse had her first birthday,

So _____ little mice were left to play.

Five little mice went out to play,

But they all came back on a sunny day.   (Five return.)

(Children substitute the number remaining each time a mouse leaves. One child at a time leaves the group. Explain singular "mouse" and plural "mice".)

53

Count One

Son counts one.

Sue counts two.

Lee counts three.

Tore counts four.

Zive counts five.

Dix counts six.

Devon counts seven.

Kate counts eight.

Tine counts nine.

Ben counts ten.

(Use only for rote counting. Volunteers choose which name they wish. When that name is called, the child counts his/her designated number.)

(Children count the number each time.)

Little Kittens

One little kitten,

Two little kittens,

Three little kittens, four.

Four little kittens,

Five little kittens

Were a cunning little brood.

One, two, three, four,

Five little kittens

There the kittens stood.

Six little kittens,

Seven little kittens

Waited for their food.

(Use as a finger play or a counting rhyme. What does cunning mean? What kinds of food do kittens like? How do you feed and take care of a kitten? What colors are kittens? What is a good name for a kitten? Do you have a pet kitten or cat? Tell about it.)

One, Two, Three

One, two, three

One, two, three

How many children

Make one, two, three?

_____ and _____ and _____ make three.

Please come and stand in front of me!

(Substitute names of children in the class. After three children respond, call upon another three until all children have had a turn. This poem can serve as an experience for roll call.)

Tall Fence Posts

One, two, one, two,
Stand up straight as fence posts do.   (Children stand tall.)

Three, four, three, four,
Crouch way down upon the floor.   (Children crouch.)

Five, six, five, six,
Nod your head and give two kicks.   (They nod heads, stand, and kick.)

Seven, eight, seven, eight,
Hold your hands and arms out straight.   (They hold arms out horizontally.)

Nine, ten, nine, ten,
Stand like fence posts once again.   (They stand tall again.)

What Comes in Pairs

A pair of mittens,   (Show hands.)
One for each hand.
A pair of boots;
Don't I look grand?   (Point to feet.)
A pair of jeans,   (Point to jeans.)
Don't they look nice?
A pair of skates,   (Point to feet.)
To zip on the ice.

*(Many children know the meaning of "pair."
Ask, "What else comes in pairs?" Sleeves, buttons, cuffs, shorts, gloves, thumbs, and so on.)*

Counting Ladybugs

One, two, three, four, five   (Point to one finger at a time.)
Five little ladybugs walk down the drive.
Their coats are shiny and bright as stars.
They look like small, newly-painted cars.
One, two, three, four, five
Five little ladybugs walk down the drive.

Two Little Squirrels

Two little squirrels
Were scampering through the wood.
Two little squirrels
Were looking for food.

Bushy Tail found two nuts,   (Hold up two fingers on one hand.)
Bright Eyes found two more.   (Hold up two fingers on other hand.)
How many nuts were there
For their winter store?

Counting to Ten

1, 2, 3, 4, 5, 6, 7, 8.	(Point to fingers one at a time.)
See me swinging on the gate.	(Lock fingers and move hands back and forth.)
1, 2, 3, 4, 5, 6, 7, 8, 9.	(Point to fingers again.)
My clothes are flopping on the line.	(Move arms back and forth.)
1, 2, 3, 4, 5, 6, 7, 8, 9, 10.	(Repeat action.)
Let us count all over again.	(Walk to seats as counting is repeated by another group.)

Animal Adventures

One little mouse, squeakety, squeak!	(Hold up one finger.)
Two little kittens, peekety, peek.	(Make motion of drawing whiskers beside mouth.)
Three little puppies, boo-woo-woo!	(Hold up three fingers.)
Four little roosters, cock-a-doodle-doo!	(Hold up four fingers.)
Five old hens, clack, clack, clack!	(Five fingers.)
Six fat ducks, quack, quack, quack.	(Six fingers.)

Counting by Two's

One bicycle goes whizzing by.	
How many wheels do you spy?	(Response.)
Two bicycles go whizzing by.	
How many wheels do you spy?	(Response.)
Three bicycles go whizzing by.	
How many wheels do you spy?	(Response.)

(Secure pictures of bicycles or draw two wheels at a time on the board so that the children can begin to learn to count by two's. Count up to six or eight for kindergarten and first graders, up to twenty for second graders.)

Rabbits Came Hopping

Three clouds are in the heavens and the sky is blue.	(Hold up three fingers and point to sky.)
Rabbits come hopping. I can see _____.	(Hold up two fingers.)
They hop to the garden and what do they see?	
A rabbit nibbling cabbage, and that makes _____.	(Hold up three fingers.)
A rabbit nibbling lettuce, and that makes _____.	(Hold up four fingers.)
1, 2, 3, 4, and are there any more?	
Yes, there are more rabbits.	
Count them—there are five.	(Hold up five fingers.)

Five bunny rabbits,

As sure as you're alive!

(Children say the missing numbers. Read Mr. Rabbit and the Lovely Presents *by Charlotte Zolotow; Harper and Row, New York, 1966.)*

Counting Things to Do

One, two, what can we do?

Three, four, let out a roar!

Five, six, stack up some bricks.

One, two, polish your shoe.

Three, four make a window and door.

Five, six, spill all of the bricks.

One, two make something new.

Three, four, sit on the floor.

Five, six, start over with bricks.

(Children can learn this rote counting rhyme easily. Ask parents to save milk cartons so that you can cover them with contact paper and use them for bricks. See that several children have at least four or five "bricks" apiece as they play this counting game. It is based upon "One, two, buckle my shoe." They may perform certain motions, such as roar like a lion, stack bricks, polish a shoe, knock down bricks, and so on. The rhyme may also be clapped from beginning to end.)

Pairs

A pair of eyes here on my face.

A pair of eyebrows right in place.

A pair of ears to hear a sound.

A pair of legs to run around.

A pair of shoulders strong and wide.

A pair of hips, one on each side.

A pair of ankles near my feet,

A pair of hands all washed and neat.

(This rhyme helps children to count by two's as they point to various parts of the body. Ask, "What else comes in pairs besides parts of the body?" Salt and pepper shakers, shoes, socks, and sleeves.)

Dive Little Goldfish

Dive, little goldfish one.   (Hold up one finger.)

Dive, little goldfish two.   (Hold up two fingers.)

Dive, little goldfish three,   (Hold up three fingers.)

Here is food, you see!   (Sprinkling motion with fingers.)

Dive, little goldfish four.   (Hold up four fingers.)

Dive, little goldfish five,   (Hold up five fingers.)

Dive, little goldfish six—   (Hold up six fingers.)

I like your funny tricks.

Six Little Girls

Six little girls/boys went out to play
Over the hills and far away.
One little girl got lost, you see,
So five little girls came home to tea.
Five little girls went out to play
Over the hills and far away.
One little girl got stung by a bee,
So four little girls came home to tea.
Continue with four, three, two, and one:

One little girl ran off to sea,
So three little girls came home to tea.
One little girl fell and hurt her knee,
So two little girls came home to tea.
One little girl lost her front door key,
So one little girl came home to tea.
End with:

"Where are the rest of the girls?" asked she,
But all of the girls came home to tea.

-Adapted from a traditional rhyme

(Six children form a set. One at a time leave the set and all return at the end of the rhyme. All the children say the rhyme with you.)

Counting at the Farm

One, one. A farm is lots of fun.
Two, two. Hear the kitten mew.
Three, three. Birds are in a tree.
Four, four. Hear the puppy snore.
Five, five. Bees buzz in a hive.

One

One is your head and one is your nose.
One is a vase for a beautiful rose.
One is the first and it comes before two.
One is a person and that is YOU!

(Ask, "How many mouths do you have? Hearts? Houses? Schools? Tongues? Mothers? Fathers? Right hands? Left hands? School buses? Desks?" Ask individuals to look in a full-length mirror and say, "I am a person.")

Counting at the Zoo

Count one, 1.
Come and have some fun!
Count two, 1, 2.
Let's run to the zoo!
Count three, 1, 2, 3.
A monkey's in a tree.
Count four, 1, 2, 3, 4.
Hear the animals roar.
Count five, 1, 2, 3, 4, 5.
Watch the porpoise dive.
Count six, 1, 2, 3, 4, 5, 6.
An ape is doing tricks.
Count seven, 1, 2, 3, 4, 5, 6, 7.
The giraffe is high as heaven.

(Suggest that the children add other animals to the zoo or substitute lines such as: "Hear the lion roar," "See the whooping crane standing in the rain," "See the big old moose. He must not get loose," "See the polar bear with white and furry hair.")

Counting Up High

One and one make two.
That I always knew.
Two and two make four.
That's a couple more.
Three and three make six.
Striped candy sticks.
Four and four make eight.
Blackbirds on the gate.
Five and five make ten.
Little finger men.
Six and six make twelve.
With a shovel delve.
Seven and seven make fourteen.
People go a-courting.
Eight and eight make sixteen.
Food my mother's mixing.
Nine and nine make eighteen.

We don't keep people waiting.

Ten and ten make twenty.

I think that is plenty.

Eleven and eleven make twenty-two.

That is enough to do.

Twelve and twelve make twenty-four.

We won't count now any more.

(This is a rote counting activity and not designed to teach the operational concept of addition. It simply is fun as "One-Two, Buckle My Shoe" is fun. Three of the couplets are not rhymed with accurate rhyming words, but this is of little consequence to the children who will enjoy the rhythm and may clap the selection. You may wish to type and duplicate the rhyme for the children to take home and share with older brothers and sisters. Discuss the meanings of couple -two or pair, delve -dig, and courting.)

Five Came Out to Play

Five little bugs came out to play.

1, 2, 3, 4, 5!

They spied a bird and they ran away.

1, 2, 3, 4, 5!

Five little birds came out for the air.

1, 2, 3, 4, 5!

They saw a cat and they flew out of there.

1, 2, 3, 4, 5!

Five little cats went out to the park.

1, 2, 3, 4, 5!

They saw a dog and were scared of his bark.

1, 2, 3, 4, 5!

Five little dogs heard a donkey cough.

1, 2, 3, 4, 5!

They turned in their tails and they scampered off.

1, 2, 3, 4, 5!

Six donkeys hid behind the trees,

When they heard the buzz of a swarm of bees.

(All children count each time and hold up five fingers. The rhyme is repetitive and easy to learn by rote. Ask, "Is every animal afraid of something? Would the bees be afraid of anything? Is

it a bad thing to be afraid?" Read "The Frightened Little Tiger" and "The Shy Little Horse" from The Wonderful Story Book *by Margaret Wise Brown; Simon and Schuster, New York, 1948.)*

Ten Huge Dinosaurs

Ten huge dinosaurs were standing in a line.

One tripped on a cobblestone and then there were _____.

Nine huge dinosaurs were trying hard to skate.

One cracked right through the ice, and then there were _____.

Eight huge dinosaurs were counting past eleven.

One counted up too far, and then there were _____.

Seven huge dinosaurs learned some magic tricks,

One did a disappearing act, and then there were _____.

Six huge dinosaurs were learning how to drive.

One forgot to put in gas, and so then there were _____.

Five huge dinosaurs joined the drum corps.

One forgot the drumsticks, and then there were _____.

Four huge dinosaurs were wading in the sea.

One waded too far out, and then there were _____.

Three huge dinosaurs looked for Mister Soo.

One gave up the search, and then there were _____.

Two huge dinosaurs went to the Amazon.

One sailed in up to his head, and then there was _____.

One lonesome dinosaur knew his friends had gone.

He found a big museum, and then there was _____.

-Adapted from an old English rhyme

(Ask, "Did you ever see dinosaur bones in a museum? Dinosaurs lived millions of years ago. There are no dinosaurs now." The class supplies the missing number. They make a set of ten and leave the set one at a time as each dinosaur dis-

appears. Suggest that they draw pictures of dinosaurs. Find a picture of one to show to the group. Discuss the meaning of the word huge. *Show something in the room that is* huge. *Compare it to something small. Discuss the meaning of "drum corps." Show the Amazon River on a map.)*

Be One, Two, Three, Four

Be one puppy trying to catch her tail.

Be two pigs that are eating from a pail.

Be three mice nibbling on some cheese.

Be four butterflies flying in the breeze.

Be five tadpoles swimming in a pool.

Be _____ boys and girls riding off to school.

Added verses:

Be one rabbit hopping up and down.

Be two squirrels hiding nuts in the ground.

Be three snow people standing in a row.

Be four roosters ready to crow.

Be five fishes splashing in a pool.

Be _____ boys and girls riding off to school.

(Individuals choose parts they wish to play as the poem is read. Substitute the number of children in the class in the last line. If used as a finger play, the children will point to a group of fingers at a time.)

60

AUTUMN DAYS

Autumn is a delightful season of colorful leaves which soon will be stripped from the trees. Flowers will soon die in their beds, hopeful of resurrection in the spring. The sun rises a little later each morning and sets a bit earlier each evening.

Birds and animals are busy preparing themselves for winter. A bluejay is perched on a tree branch scolding everyone for not allowing summer to continue. Bushy-tailed squirrels will not forgot where they buried nuts in preparation for a possible famine. They take bundles of leaves and grasses up to the forks of trees where they will make nests.

A mouse is shredding papery bark from stems to make a winter nest and she cunningly hides it in the undergrowth for the present. The groundhog is creeping sleepily along looking for a place where he can hide and sleep for the winter. Hornet's nests are deserted. The last of the fruit hangs on branches in the orchards.

People will soon be thinking about anti-freeze and snow tires for their cars. Beach houses will soon be deserted and fields are already bare. In the evenings we settle in front of a blazing fire in the fireplace and at bedtime snuggle down under extra blankets. Soon the earth will be covered with whiteness, but for now autumn is here, autumn is here, a most colorful season of the year!

September

Autumn is near, and September is here.

What will boys and girls do

When the weather is cool?

Will they swim in a pool?

Will they make up a rule?

Will they shout, "April Fool?" NO!

They will get on a bus

When the weather is cool,

Say goodbye to us

And they'll ride off to school.

Yes, ride off to school!

Packing a Lunch for School

I am packing my lunch

And I have a hunch

That I'll have a boiled egg,   (Make small circle with fingers.)

And a chicken leg,   (Hold up pointer finger.)

With two slices of bread,   (Hold up two fingers.)

And an apple red.   (Make circle with thumbs and forefingers.)

And some milk to drink,   (Pretend to drink.)

And a cookie pink,   (Make small circle.)

And a pickle or two,

And some nuts to chew,

What a lunch this will be!

Will you share it with me?

At School

We play a lot of games

And we learn each other's names.

We count to ten or more,   (Count to ten.)

And make a grocery store.   (Pretend to build with blocks.)

We learn our ABC's   (Say as many as possible—perhaps half.)

We make three sets of threes.   (Put three small objects in three sets made of a circle of string.)

And a puppet from a bag.   (Work hand up and down.)

And then salute the flag.   (Hand over heart.)

We listen and we write   (Pretend to write.)

We read and we recite.

I just cannot remember

All I learn in September!

Autumn is Here

Autumn is here; autumn is here!

The little gray squirrels tell us

Autumn is here.   (Children say this.)

Autumn is here; autumn is here!

The golden leaves tell us that

Autumn is here!

Autumn is here; autumn is here!

The cool breezes tell us that

Autumn is here!

(Words are repetitive and children can learn the poem easily. Ask, "What else tells us that autumn is here? Why would you wear warmer clothes? Where do the birds go now that they can build no nests?")

Little Seed

Dear little seed, so soft and round

You may rest down under the ground.

Inside this hole you may safely hide.

You must stay there and not peep outside.

I've dug a small place and I've laid you down.

Your leaves will come up,

And your roots will go down.

(Children crouch to the floor and cover eyes. Gradually, they rise, spreading legs for roots and spreading arms to represent full grown plants.)

Five Old Crows

Five old crows were on a brick wall.

Four were tall and the other was small.

One old crow cried, "Caw, caw, caw!"

He went to visit his mother-in-law.

Four old crows were on a brick wall.

Three were tall and the other was small.

One old crow went to get some food.

He never came back to the other brood.

Three old crows were on a brick wall.

Two were tall and the other was small.

The small one grew and grew and grew.

He flew away and that left two.

Two old crows were on a brick wall.

Both were old and both of them tall.

One crow said, "I miss my son."

He flew away and that left one.

One old crow was on a brick wall.

He flew away and there was the wall!

One brick wall was alone in the rain,

Wishing for the crows to come back again.

-Adapted from an old English rhyme

(Five children line up on a row of blocks that simulate a wall. One "crow" at a time flies away and all children may say the refrain. Continue

62

the action by using five more children until each child has had a turn. This rhyme may be used as a finger play as children bend down one finger at a time. Ask, "Do you think the crows ever came back? Why? Make up a story about the Happy Wall. When the old crows returned, what happened? Do you like the way the rhyme ended? Can you think of another ending?")

Popcorn

Rub an ear of corn hard as you can, can, can.   (Rhythm may be clapped on repeated words.)

Put every yellow kernel in the pan, pan, pan.

Put the popcorn popper on the flame, flame, flame

And listen for the popping in the game, game, game.

1, 2, 3, 4, 5. Give a shake, shake, shake.   (Children count.)

6, 7, 8, 9, 10. Noise they make, make, make!   (Children count.)

Inside the popper they will pop, pop, pop.

Hold the lid or outside they will hop, hop, hop.

1, 2, 3, 4, 5. I count them once again.   (Hold up five fingers.)

But I will count no more after 6, 7, 8, 9, 10.   (Hold up fingers on opposite hand.)

Every yellow grain will turn to white, white, white.

Open up the popper! What a sight, sight, sight.

Now that all the popping is all right, right, right,

Fill the bowl and then we'll have a bite, bite, bite.

(Bring in an electric stove and give the children an experience at popping corn. After a first reading, the class will be able to say all repetitive words with you. Popcorn in a foil pan can be purchased at most supermarkets. Provide paper drinking cups for each child to fill.)

Scarecrow

Out in the meadow

A scarecrow stood.   (Stand stiff with arms outstretched.)

His body was a stuffed coat.

His legs were made of wood.

His head had a straw hat   (Hands on top of head.)

Very large and round.   (Make circle with arms.)

His arms were two broom sticks   (Hold up arms straight.)

63

And his feet were on the ground.   (Stamp feet.)

His coat had ragged patches   (Hands on thighs.)

They were faded and worn out.

He frightened all the crows   (Flap arms up and down.)

That were flying all about.

You simply won't believe this,

But I will tell you that

Some birds had made a straw nest

Inside of his hat.   (Cup hands for nest.)

(Use four cardboard tubes from tissue and a longer one for the body. Cut tubes in proportion to arms and legs. Roll paper around the tube used for a head. Fasten the pieces together with paper fasteners. Suggest that children cut scraps of fabric and "dress" the scarecrow. Use materials from the odds and ends box. Attach straws inside legs so that the scarecrow can stand.)

The Three Crows

One shiny crow sat up in a tree.

Caw, caw, caw!   (Children repeat.)

Two shiny crows were as fat as could be.

Caw, caw, caw!

Three shiny crows ate from early morn.

Caw, caw, caw!

They ate every ear of the farmer's fresh corn.

Caw, caw, caw!

The scarecrow danced, and they all flew away

Caw, caw, caw!

And said they would come back again next day.

Caw, caw, caw!

(Children hold up one finger at a time to represent the crows. The entire class says the refrain. Ask, "Show us on the calendar 'next day.' Why did the crows leave the cornfield?")

Counting Tumbleweeds

Ten little tumbleweeds were by the corral gate.

The wind whooshed two away and then there were _____.

Eight little tumbleweeds said, "Oh, fiddlesticks!"

Two danced with the wind and then there were _____.

Six little tumbleweeds heard the wild wind roar.

Two were whirled far away and then there were _____.

Four little tumbleweeds were waiting for their cue.

A gentle breeze blew two away and then there were _____.

Two little tumbleweeds, round and round they spun

Until they were out of sight and then there was _____.

(This rhyme emphasizes subtracting by two's. Bend down two fingers at a time or use feathers for tumbleweeds, asking individuals to remove two at a time as the rhyme is said by the class. Concepts and vocabulary: cue, corral gate, spun - not spinned.)

Three Little Oak Leaves

Three little oak leaves, red, yellow, gold,

Were happy when the weather turned cold.

One said, "I'll make a coat for an elf

So that he will be able to warm himself."

One said, "I'll make a home for a bug,

So that she will be safe as a bug in a rug."

One said, "I'll cover a seed in the ground

Till spring, it will be very safe and sound."

Three little oak leaves, red, yellow, gold

Were happy when the weather turned cold.

(Counting and subtracting by two's. Bend down two fingers at a time or use real leaves in a string set, and ask a child to remove two at a time as the rhyme is said. Review rhyming words: "What rhymes with gold? with himself? with rug? and with sound?")

Special Hats

A pointed hat for Halloween,   (Place two pointer fingers together.)

My witch won't go without.

A firefighter wears a helmet,   (Hands clasped above heads.)

And puts the fires out.

A scarecrow's hat is made of straw.   (Sway body and place hands held widely apart over head.)

He doesn't care for style.   (Measure tallness over head.)

A handkerchief and tall black hat

Will make my snowman smile.

Busy Squirrel

The little gray squirrel makes a scampering   (Wiggle fingers.)
sound

As she gathers the nuts that fall to the ground. (Hold fingers high and let them move as they descend.)

She buries the nuts in a secret dark place   (One hand over other.)

And covers them over with hardly a trace.

Little gray squirrels always seem to know

That the robins have gone and it's time for snow. (Raise arms and let fingers move as they descend.)

Raking Leaves

I rake the leaves   (Motion of raking.)

When they fall down   (Raise arms and let fingers fall gradually.)

In a great big pile.   (Measure.)

And when there are enough of them,

I jump on them awhile.   (Give three jumps.)

66

Our Tenth Month

Wear a warm coat for fall is here.	
It is the tenth month of the year.	(Hold up ten fingers.)
One for the cornfield,	(Hold up one finger.)
Two for the leaves,	(Hold up two fingers.)
Three for the cold rain that drips from the eaves.	(Hold up three fingers.)
Four for the ponds that soon will freeze,	(Hold up four fingers.)
And five for empty bird's nests in the trees.	(Hold up five fingers.)
Wear a warm coat for autumn is here.	
It is the tenth month of the year.	(Hold up ten fingers.)

A Leaf of Gold

One leaf of gold, two leaves of brown
Upon the ground came tumbling down.
Three leaves of green, four leaves of red,
Came tumbling down upon my head.
Five yellow leaves sailed through the air
And softly fell upon my hair.
The leaves of brown, and leaves of gold
Are more than my two arms can hold.
And while I stand beneath the tree,
A thousand leaves fall down on me.

(Hold up the correct number of fingers. When leaves tumble, raise arms and lower moving fingers. Ask, "Show with your fingers how leaves would tumble. How would they sail?")

Fall Leaves

One leaf and two leaves
Tumbling to the ground,
Three leaves and four leaves
Make a rustling sound.
Five leaves and six leaves
Twirling all around,
Seven leaves and eight leaves
Whirling in a mound.
Nine leaves and ten leaves—
A north wind comes along,
And blows every leaf away
And that ends my song!

(Use as a finger play. Place cut-out construction paper leaves on the flannelboard for counting. Ask children to pretend to be leaves. As the North Wind blows, they scurry to their seats. Suggest that children bring in leaves and discuss their colors, shapes, and textures.)

67

The Nut Tree

Five brown chestnuts fell from the tree.	(Hold up five fingers.)
I thought that the chestnuts were only for me.	
But one was taken home by a girl.	(Hold up four fingers.)
And one was taken home by a squirrel.	(Hold up three fingers.)
A chipmunk took one to her nest.	(Hold up two fingers.)
I hurried up and took all the rest.	(Hold up one finger.)
I planted one nearby, you see.	
Some day, we'll have a new nut tree!	(Raise arm high.)

Five Juicy Apples

Five juicy apples grew upon a tree.	(Place five apple cutouts on flannelboard.)
I looked right at them and they looked back at me.	
I picked one apple and I put it in a sack.	
I took it to school and I had it for a snack.	(Remove an apple.)
Now there are four,	
And not one more.	
Four juicy apples!	
A bird came along, and she ate her fill.	
She pecked at an apple with her little yellow bill.	(Remove an apple.)
Now there are three	
As you can see	
Three juicy apples!	

68

A pony came by and he was very tall.

He picked one apple and he ate it leaves and all.   (Remove an apple.)

Now there are two;

But we're not through.

Two juicy apples!

A bear came along and he climbed up the tree.

He said, "Woof, woof! Here's an apple for me!"   (Remove an apple.)

Now there is one.

We'll soon be done.

One juicy apple!

One red apple decided not to stay.

It fell from the tree and it rolled far away.   (Remove an apple.)

Now we are done,

For there are none.

No juicy apples!

Three Ships

There were three ships, one, two, and three:

The Nina, the Pinta, and Santa Marie.   (Hold up a finger for each ship.)

Over the ocean, over the sea,   (Make wavy motions with hands.)

The Nina, the Pinta, the Santa Marie.

Columbus discovered a land so new,

And that was in 1492.

There was many a mile, and the ships were three:

The Nina, the Pinta, the Santa Marie.

                                    -Olive Amundson

Columbus and the Three Ships

Three ships sailed from the shores of Spain,

Over the seas and back again,

In the Nina, the Pinta, and the Santa Marie.   (Hold up a finger for each ship.)

Columbus was clever and very smart

To sail three ships with stars for a chart:

The Nina, the Pinta, the Santa Marie.

Christopher Columbus and his band

Found their way to an unknown land

With the Nina, the Pinta, and the Santa Marie.

69

HALLOWEEN

Halloween is scary but fun for children. Its customs are two thousand years old. In older times, October 31 was a time when the year ended, for nature seemed to be dying. Leaves and flowers withered and plants drooped. Black cats were thought to be evil and have great powers as witches' helpers. Many of the old customs have been carried over to the present time.

Now Halloween is a dress-up time. Children parade in costumes and go from door to door ringing doorbells and saying, "Trick or treat." They carry jack o'lanterns up and down the street. Games are enjoyed in the household. Popcorn is popped, chestnuts are roasted, and apples are shared, just as in olden days of the Druids. From this sharing came the sharing of treats.

But Halloween is the evening before the first day of November. Soon the flaming hillsides will be covered with blankets of white snow.

Four Little Owls

This little owl has great, round eyes.   (Point to one finger at a time.)

This little owl is of very small size.

This little owl can turn her head.

This little owl likes mice, she said.

This little owl flies all around,

And her wings make hardly a single sound.

(Pretend a desk or table is the tree. One child is the owl; another, the sun. The owl sleeps. The sun goes down. The owl awakens and flies away to look for mice to feed her babies. The sun comes up and the owl goes back to her "tree.")

Halloween Time

Halloween will soon be here.

It is now that time of year.

Can you be a big black cat?

Arch your back? Spit, spat, spat!   (Make arch of arm.)

Can you be a pumpkin bright.

And smile at me all through the night?   (Make circle with arms.)

Can you be a feathery owl

And look at me with a great big scowl?   (Children frown.)

Can you be a scary ghost

Dancing all around a post?   (Flop arms.)

BOO!

(Discuss Halloween etiquette. Ask, "What do we say when people give us treats? How many times should you ring a doorbell?"-Once. Suggest that

children choose costumes that can be seen by drivers as they go from house to house quietly. "Be sure to wear a mask that does not cover the eyes. Save all of the treats not eaten. Help younger children keep Halloween rules.")

One Jack O'Lantern Stares

One jack o'lantern that I see

Is quietly staring right at me.

The witch rides by with her pet cat.

The jack o'lantern stares at that.

An owl is sitting on a limb.

The jack o'lantern stares at him.

A little bat has velvet fur.

The jack o'lantern stares at her.

There comes a ghost all dressed in white.

The jack o'lantern stares all night.

At night, the jack o'lantern stares.

It's Halloween, and no one cares!

(Children may choose the character they wish to play. The jack o'lantern sits staring straight ahead. The witch pretends to ride a broom. The owl hoots, the bat flies by. The ghost flutters. All of the class will say the second line of each couplet.)

Little Ghosts

The first little ghost floated by the store.

The second little ghost stood outside the door.

The third little ghost tried her best to hide.

The fourth little ghost stood by my side.

The fifth little ghost near the window sill

Gave everybody a great big thrill.

The five little ghosts were all my friends,

And that is the way that this story ends.

(Make puppet ghosts by rolling up a ball of newspaper, laying a large square of white sheeting over it, and tying at the neck. Draw eyes and mouth with a black felt-tip pen.)

71

Five Girls and Boys

Five girls and boys were dressed like ghosts

Hiding behind dark fences and posts.

The first one gave a terrible roar.

She scared herself, dropped her sheet,

Then there were ———.

The second one said, "Oh, fiddle-dee-dee!

I've lost my mask and my sheet!"

Then there were ———.

The third one jumped and lost her right shoe.

She lost her sheet. Oh, dear me!

Then there were ———.

The fourth one said, "I'm going to run!"

But he tripped on his sheet,

And then there was ———.

The fifth one laughed and thought it was fun.

He fell down, lost his sheet,

And then there was ———.

Well, they just couldn't miss all those goodies to eat,

So each boy and girl went home to get another sheet.

(Pupils supply the remaining number. Review ordinal concepts: first, second, and so on. Invite children to choose lines to dramatize. Ask: "Show how you would drop your sheet and run." Bring in some discarded white sheets and use them for ghost play. Read part of a line and ask the class to supply the rest and the rhyming word until they are familiar enough to say the words or act out the rhyme.)

Pumpkin Head

My head is round,

And so are my eyes.

My nose is a triangle,

Just this size.

My mouth is turned up

Like a shiny half-moon.

Upon your front porch

I'll be sitting quite soon.

Upon your front porch,

There I will be seen

Smiling at children

On this Halloween!

(Bring in a pumpkin. Cut off the top. The children will enjoy scooping out the seeds and helping you make a jack o'lantern. To dramatize, ask the class to form a round head with arms, point fingers to make a triangle shape, and draw a half-moon in the air. Concepts to be discussed are: round, triangle, and half-moon. After you have read the poem two or three times, the children can dramatize it with you.)

Three Little Witches

One little, two little, three little witches   (Hold up fingers one by one.)

Ride through the sky on a broom.   (Move head quickly through air.)

One little, two little, three little witches   (Hold up fingers again.)

Wink their eyes at the moon.   (Wink one eye while making circle with arms.)

Here is a Witch's Tall Black Hat

Here is a witch's tall black hat.   (Point index fingers together.)

Here are the whiskers on her cat.   (Index fingers and thumbs are put together and pulled back and forth under nose.)

Here is an owl sitting in a tree.   (Circle eyes with fingers.)

Here is a goblin! Hee, hee, hee!   (Hold hand on stomach area.)

(Ask pupils to pretend to be Halloween cats walking along a fence. They hold arms out at sides and step with one foot directly in front of the other. Draw a chalk line on the floor for this activity.)

Five Green Goblins

Five green goblins

Danced on Halloween.

Two were fat, two were thin,

And one was in between.

The first green goblin danced upon his toes.

The second green goblin bumped his funny nose.

The third green goblin hurried through the town.

The fourth green goblin acted like a clown.

The fifth green goblin sang a goblin tune.

Then five green goblins danced beneath the moon.

(You may use as a finger play or the children may dramatize the actions, choosing goblins to act out the parts. Sing "Three Green Goblins" from More Singing Fun *by Lucille F. Wood and Louise Binder Scott; Bowmar/Noble Publishers, Los Angeles, 1954.)*

Four Big Jack O'Lanterns

Four big jack o'lanterns made a funny sight

Sitting on a gate post Halloween night.

Number one said, "I see a witch's hat!"

Number two said, "I see a big, black cat!"

Number three said, "I see a scary ghost!"

Number four said, "By that other post!"

Four big jack o'lanterns weren't a bit afraid.

They marched right along in the Halloween parade.

(Point to one finger at a time. Bring in a pumpkin and discuss how a jack o'lantern is made. Suggest that children draw and color jack o'lanterns with different expressions: happy, sad, angry, and so on. If they have heard the rhyme once or twice, individuals may say the words in quotations. On the last line, they march around the rug or teacher's desk. If you want to drill on ordinals, change to the first, second, third, and fourth jack o'lanterns. Ask, "Why weren't the jack o'lanterns afraid?")

Why We Have Jack O'Lanterns

Did you know that jack o'lanterns

Are of Indian breed?

That the Indian gave the white people

Their first pumpkin seed?

That the Indian kids cut faces

In the golden rind?

Some quite ugly, some quite jolly,

Some of every kind?

The children made some happy

With a merry grin.

Then to make them human,

They put a bright light in.

That is how a jack o'lantern

You have often seen

Was made, so thank the Indians

For every Halloween.

        -Adapted from an Unknown Author

On Halloween Night

One witch is riding on a broom

Two spooks are walking near my room.

Three hoot owls on the roof call, "Who!"

Four little goblins answer, "Boo!"

I see a friendly, shining moon

As big and round as a balloon.

Soon I will go out on the street

With (children, Daddy, Mother) for my trick or treat.

(Talk about Halloween safety. Use as a counting rhyme or finger play. Choose ten children to dramatize the action. Read Tell Me, Mr. Owl *by Doris Van Liew Foster; Lathrop, Lee and Shepard, New York, 1957.)*

A Halloween Happening

The sky was dark but a moon was seen.

And a little owl hooted, "Halloween!"

Two velvety bats flew down with a flop.

Three goblins pranced with a hippety-hop.

Four cats jumped up on a witch's broom.

The four cats didn't have lots of room.

Five hoot owls fluttered and flew around.

Making a soft and fluttering sound.

The witch took off with an ala-ka-zoom!

And the four black cats fell off of the broom.

Two bats looked on; three goblins did, too.

Four black cats sat and cried, "Mew, mew."

Five white ghosts made a frightful scene

And one little owl hooted, "Halloween!"

      -Adapted from an old rhyme.

(Ask, "Why did the witch leave four cats behind? What did she say to them? Supposing the witch returned. Make up a little play about the witch's return. Tell what the goblin said to her; the owls; the cats." The children may make paper bag masks from large paper bags that fit over the head. They cut eyes, nose, and mouth openings and decorate their masks with materials from the odds and ends box.)

(Repeat owl sound and flap wings.)

(Motion of flapping wings and falling without sound.)

(Children hippety-hop.)

(Children say, "Meow".)

(Children stand close together.)

(Fly softly.)

(Children hoot.)

(Witch grabs broom and cats sit on the floor.)

Dressed Up for Halloween

An old witch laughed, "Hee, hee, hee, hee!"
And then she waved goodby.
She rode her long thin broomstick
That was pointed toward the sky.
She moved her crooked fingers
With her long sharp fingernails.
Two black cats meowed and meowed at her
And fluffed their furry tails.
Three skeletons did a creaky dance,
And whispered, "Ee-ee-ee-ee!"
Four feathery owls flew all around,
And went back to their tree.
Five white ghosts slithered here and there
Like fishes in the sea.
We were all dressed in costumes,
And one costume was for me.

(This rhyme may be used for dramatization with fifteen children playing the Halloween characters. Read the rhyme first and ask, "How would skeletons do a creaky dance? How would ghosts slither by? How would a witch gallop on her broomstick? Tell us." Then ask the children to volunteer for parts to act out. Suggest that they say as many of the words in the rhyme as they can remember. Select a second group of children so that everyone has a turn. The children can make sack masks or use clothing from the dress-up box for costumes. Read Good-Night, Owl by Pat Hutchins; Macmillan, New York, 1972.)

Sounds and Sights on Halloween

The first girl/boy said, "It's a very dark sky."
The second one said, "Shapes go hurrying by."
The third one said, "I hear creaks and moans."
The fourth one said, "I hear goblin groans."
The fifth one said, "Spooky sights are seen,
Because, my dear, it is Halloween!"

(Use as a finger play for the teaching of ordinals. Listen for "th" at the end of fourth and fifth.)

Disappearing Witches

Five little witches on Halloween night
Came out to play when the moon was bright.
One took a broom and thumped on my door.
She flew away, and then there were _____.
One did a witch's dance near the oak tree.
She flew away and then there were _____.
One swished her costume and made a loud
BOO!
She flew away and then there were _____.
One scared a goblin and that was great fun.
She flew away and then there was _____.
The last little witch combed her long, thin hair.
She jumped on her broom and whizzed through the air.

(The children supply the number. They choose which witch they want to be and dramatize the rhyme. Each "witch" flies away and leaves the set.)

THANKSGIVING

The first Thanksgiving was celebrated by the Pilgrims in 1621 after they had gathered their first harvest. The year before, they had come on the Mayflower to set up their homes in a new world. After a cold and hungry winter, they had planted crops. On the first Thanksgiving, they gave thanks to God that their crops had prospered. The Pilgrims celebrated Thanksgiving for three days. Ninety Indians came to join them. The Indians brought game.

In 1863, President Abraham Lincoln made a proclamation setting aside the last Thursday in November as a day for Thanksgiving. Now Thanksgiving is one of our American legal holidays like Christmas or the Fourth of July.

Five Little Pilgrims

There were five little Pilgrims on Thanksgiving Day: (Hold up five fingers.)

The first one said, "I'll have cake if I may."

The second one said, "I'll have turkey roasted."

The third one said, "I'll have chestnuts toasted."

The fourth one said, "I will have pumpkin pie."

The fifth one said, "I'll have jam by and by."

But before they had any turkey and dressing,

The Pilgrims all said a Thanksgiving blessing.

(Make a "thankful" book. In the book each child pastes a picture of something for which he/she is thankful. Write the child's name under the picture.)

Thanksgiving Dinner

Thanksgiving Day will soon be here,

And I can hardly wait

To see two turkey drumsticks brown   (Hold up two fingers.)

Heaped up upon my plate.

And mashed potatoes in three bowls.   (Hold up three fingers.)

Four spicy pumpkin pies,   (Hold up four fingers.)

Five bowls of turkey dressing,   (Hold up five fingers.)

And six jars of jam this size.   (Hold up six fingers.)

Seven tasty kinds of cakes,   (Hold up seven fingers.)

And cookies, chocolate chip,

And ice cream in a freezer,

We'll have more than one dip.   (Cup hands.)

Eight bowls of squash and peas and beans,

(Hold up eight fingers.)

Nine loaves of crusty bread,

(Hold up nine fingers.)

Ten bowls of yummy gravy,

(Hold up ten fingers.)

And one dish of cranberries red.

Thanksgiving is the day we feast,

And gather all our brood

To say that we are thankful

For friends and home and food.

(Children will enjoy pictures of a Thanksgiving dinner. Encourage conversation.)

The First Thanksgiving

T is for Turkey all roasted and brown.

H is for Harvest moon shining down.

(Make circle with arms.)

A is for Apple pie so juicy to eat.

(Make smaller circle with fingers.)

N is for Nuts that make a nice treat.

(Make very small circle with two fingers.)

K is for Kitchen where we stir the cake.

(Make smaller circular motion for stirring.)

S is for Soup which we always make.

(Make shape of bowl with hands.)

G is for Guests we greet when we meet.

(Shake hands with a friend.)

I is for Ice cream so cold and so sweet.

(Pretend to lick spoon.)

V is for Vegetables tasty and good.

I is for Indians that shared all their food.

N is for November that soon will be here.

(Show on calendar.)

G is for Glad for our blessings each year.

(Hands clasped.)

(Write this acrostic on the board vertically. Read the poem to the class and ask, "Do you have enough fingers for all of the letters? How many fingers would you need? Perhaps you can help me say the rhyme. If you can remember the name that goes with the alphabet letter, I will write the name on the board after we say the line.")

I am Thankful

I am thankful for pets.

I am thankful for school.

I am thankful when I

Can swim in a pool.

I am thankful for home,

And the food that I eat.

I am thankful for all

The new friends that I meet.

I am thankful for health,

And for my family

I'm especially thankful

That I am just ME!

(Ask: "Could anybody in this class have written this poem? Does it say what you might have said about being thankful? Tell us something for which you are thankful and I will write it on the board. Why are you glad that you are YOU? Did you pronounce the first sound in the word thankful? *Say the word with me:* thankful. *Show me something in this room for which you are thankful.")*

Turkey Walk

Old turkey gobbler walks very proudly;

Gobble, gobble, gobble,

Strut, strut, strut!

When he walks, he gobbles very loudly:

Gobble, gobble, gobble,

Strut, strut, strut!

Hold your head high if you please,

Gobble, gobble, gobble,

Strut, strut, strut!

And when you walk, don't bend your knees.

Gobble, gobble, gobble,

Strut, strut, strut!

(Children repeat.)

(Children hold heads high and walk stiff-legged.)

Thanksgiving Pies

A baker made ten round pies

From his recipe.

"Oh, they are full of fruit and spice—

Delicious pies," said he.

Then Mister Baker sold one pie to Mrs. Anna Dell.

How many lovely juicy pies would there be left to sell?

If Mister Baker sold two pies to Mrs. Arthur Wise,

(Make circle with hands.)

(Nine.)

That would leave how many round Thanksgiving pies?   (Seven.)

How many pies would be left when Mr. David Skinner

Came to buy two of the pies for his Thanksgiving dinner?   (Five.)

Mrs. Ober bought one pie—just one pie and no more,

For a picnic in the hills, and that would leave just _____.   (Four.)

Mister Baker sold one pie to Mr. Otto Price.

That would leave how many pies so full of fruit and spice?   (Three.)

How many pies now would there be, if one pie he did sell

To two hungry little boys? How many? Can you tell?   (Two.)

If Mister Baker gave two pies to pretty little Jenny,

How many pies did he have left? Did he have none or many?   (None.)

(The children supply the remaining number each time the baker sells pies. Use also for a study of the community.)

Three Turkey Gobblers

The day before Thanksgiving, as quiet as could be,

Three turkey gobblers sat up in a tree.   (Hold up three fingers.)

The first turkey said, "I think that I will hide

Out behind the haystack for it is tall and wide."   (Point to one finger at a time.)

The second turkey said, "I'll stay here in this tree,

And hide behind some branches where no one can see me."

The third turkey said, "I think I'll leave today,

For then the cook can't find me and put me on a tray."

And on Thanksgiving morning, when the farmer came to call,

The three turkey gobblers could not be found at all.

(The children may dramatize the poem rather than use it as an action rhyme. Find a large picture of a turkey and paste it on cardboard. Punch two holes and draw strings through them. Individuals may volunteer to wear it around the neck and say, "Gobble, gobble, gobble" when someone talks to her/him. Let a number of children take turns.)

This Turkey Gobbler

This turkey gobbler spreads his tail.   (Spread fingers on both hands.)

It looks like a fan and it helps him sail.

This turkey gobbler chases a cat.   (Hold up one finger at a time.)

He runs so fast that he falls down flat.   (Clap.)

This turkey gobbler with wattles of red

Chases a puppy, but can't get ahead.

This turkey gobbler makes a strange noise:

Gobble, gobble, gobble at the girls and boys.   (Children make sound.)

This turkey gobbler just loves to chase.

He will not hurt me for he likes the race!

All turkey gobblers have angry looks,

For they are afraid of the ovens and the cooks!

Pumpkins and Turkeys

Five yellow pumpkins side by side

Wanted to run away and hide.

Five turkey gobblers all in a row,

Said, "Hop on our backs and away we'll go!"

Five yellow pumpkins and the turkeys, too,

On Thanksgiving Day, away they flew.

One, two, three, four, five, six, seven,

Eight, nine, ten, up toward heaven.

The man in the moon laughed, "Ho, ho, ho!

I think they were very wise to go!"

(Place five pumpkin shapes on the flannelboard. Then place five turkey shapes below the pumpkins. On the line, "Hop on our backs," place pumpkins on top of turkeys. Add a happy moon face.)

Turkey in the Straw

Turkey in the straw and turkey in the pan.

I am saying, "Thank you" as nicely as I can.

Turkey in the oven, turkey in the hay,

All I want is turkey on Thanksgiving Day.

-Traditional

(Do the turkey walk. Hold head high and walk with stiff legs.)

Pilgrim Children

Pilgrim children did not play

On that first Thanksgiving Day.

The first chopped wood which he would take

To help his sister cook and bake.

The second took a great big sack,

80

And brought some nuts; all they could crack.

The third one got a turkey and

She helped to roast it in a pan.

The fourth ground corn to make some bread.

The fifth made covers for the bed.

The sixth one brought a pumpkin by

She cut it up to make a pie.

The seventh came and popped some corn.

The eighth fed horses in the barn.

The ninth watched food or it might burn.

The tenth churned butter in a churn.

Pilgrim children did not play

On that first Thanksgiving Day.

(Bring in children's books concerning Pilgrims, Indians, and Thanksgiving for the browsing table. Although this rhyme is long, its various words can be discussed, "Why would the first child chop wood? Where would the second child get walnuts? What would have to be done to the turkey before it could be roasted?" Describe an old-fashioned churn and tell how butter was made. Ask, "Why did Pilgrim children have so much work to do? Would you like to be a Pilgrim child? Why?" As a memory test ask, "What did the first Pilgrim do? What did the second Pilgrim gather? What did the fourth one grind? What did the sixth one do with a pumpkin?")

Five Yellow Pumpkins

The first yellow pumpkin said, "Oh, my!
I don't want to be a pumpkin pie."

      (Hold up one finger at a time.)

The second yellow pumpkin said, "Oh, dear!
Something will happen to us, I fear."

The third yellow pumpkin said, "Oh, me!
I am as frightened as I can be."

The fourth yellow pumpkin said, "Let's go!
I won't be a jack o'lantern! No, no, no!"

The fifth yellow pumpkin said, "It's late!
I fear I will be served upon a plate."

The five yellow pumpkins rolled far away,
And could not be found Thanksgiving Day.

The man in the moon said, "Hooray for you!
It was time to go, and I'm glad you knew."

HOLIDAYS IN DECEMBER

Holidays touch the culture of home and every nation of the world. They enrich the lives of individuals and give cohesiveness to society. People of different cultures understand the purposes for particular festivities and beliefs and realize that many of them overlap.

Holidays are cherished in the United States and have become a yearly tradition. From them, esteem and foundations for patriotism and love of country can be built.

HOW CHRISTMAS IS CELEBRATED

Santa Claus is strictly American. European children have other visitors.

Dutch children watch for St. Nicholas, a tall man with a white beard, dressed in a bishop's robe and a tall pointed hat. He comes on December 3, St. Nicholas Eve. On that evening, children put their shoes before the fireplace. They stuff hay and carrots into the shoes for St. Nicholas' horse. When Dutch settlers came to the new world, they brought St. Nicholas with them. If you try to say the words St. Nicholas very fast, you can almost hear "Santa Claus".

Swedish children look forward to St. Lucy's Day which is December 13, and this day leads to Christmas. A girl wearing a crown of pine boughs and seven lighted candles awakens the family and serves them cakes and coffee. On Christmas an imaginary white-bearded dwarf brings gifts in a sleigh.

Danish children have a mysterious visitor named Jule Nesse, a kind old man who supposedly lives in an attic. On Christmas Eve, the children put porridge and milk for him at the door of the attic.

Spanish children look for three callers. On New Year's Eve, visitors dressed as the three Wise Men may appear. The children put hay in their own shoes for the Wise Men's camels.

Italian children look for an old gnome or sprite the twelfth night after Christmas. They have a manger and a star.

Puerto Rican children enjoy twelve days of Christmas and believe in Santa Claus. Before the children go to sleep, they hang their stockings at the head of the bed.

Hebrew children celebrate Hanukkah.

Alaska celebrates Christmas at night.

Ozark children are told that cows kneel at midnight to worship the Christ Child.

Hawaiian children display Santa Claus.

CHRISTMAS IN MEXICO

Christmas begins in Mexico on December 16 and ends with the observance of Epiphany, January 6.

Many Mexican families share in the work of preparing for the Christmas season. After they have finished their work, these Mexican families load all of their treasures in cars and go to the cities to sell their wares.

In every city there are puestos or market stalls. Across the front of each stall are hung piñatas.

The celebration of La Posada begins on December 16 and continues for nine nights, the last night on Christmas Eve. The families may observe La Posada by meeting at nine different family homes on nine different nights; or they may celebrate at the same house with only the family present.

82

La Posada begins with a recitation of the rosary by the head of the house. Then children carry lighted candles and march around the house. The children leading the procession carry images of Mary and Joseph. At the door of each room, they will beg for admission to the "Inn," but are turned away. Finally, they reach the room where an altar is seen. This is the stable they may enter. There is a manger in the stable but it always stays empty until Christmas Eve.

Following religious ceremonies is the breaking of the piñata. Finally broken, it contains goodies of every kind and small toys or whistles.

On Christmas Eve, the Babe is placed in the manger and everyone sings praises to the Infant.

Singing, dancing, and fireworks are seen with another piñata and attendence of mass at church.

Mexican children write letters to the Christ Child, listing their wishes for gifts. They place their shoes at the foot of the bed the night of Epiphany, January 6.

One Is for the Manger

One is for the manger   (Hold up one finger.)
Where Baby Jesus lay.

Two for Mary and Joseph   (Hold up two fingers.)
On that Christmas Day.

Three is for the wise men   (Hold up three fingers.)
Who brought three gifts of love.

Four is for the shepherds   (Hold up four fingers.)
And angel songs above.

Five is for the animals   (Hold up five fingers.)
Who stood guard in the shed

Over Baby Jesus   (Make arc of arms.)
In His manger bed.

A Story that Never Grows Old

Once a little Baby lay   (Two hands at side of head.)
Sleeping in a manger,
Resting on a bed of hay,
A precious little Stranger.
Shepherds on the hillside stayed
With their sheep at night;
Heard sweet strains of music played;   (Hand behind ear.)
Saw a heavenly light.   (Point upward.)
The donkeys and the cows stood near.   (Hold up two fingers on each hand for ears.)
Wise men came from far.
Mary held the Baby dear;   (Motion of cradling.)
Over them a star.   (Point to heavens.)
Wise men came themselves to know   (Hold up three fingers.)
Of the Baby's birth.
Wise men knelt on bended knee.   (Kneel and fold hands.)
Christ had come to earth!

The Piñata

My goodness! My goodness!
A big paper jar!   (Make large circle with hands.)
A big paper jar that is shaped like a star.   (Draw star shape in air.)
And filled full of walnuts and filled full of   (Cup hands.)
sweets,
Of toys and of oranges and wonderful treats.
Let's hit it and hit it and hit it until   (Pretend to hit piñata.)
The piñata breaks and makes everything spill! (Clap.)
OLE!   (Children cry "Olé" and scramble to pick up goodies.)

(Ask your Spanish-speaking children to describe a piñata and tell about their experiences at breaking one.)

Hanukkah Time

Hanukkah's coming. It's coming tonight.
I have shined our Menorah all splendidly bright,
With eight pretty candles to give us some light.   (Show eight fingers.)
The Hanukkah season has just now begun
With pancakes and presents for everyone,
Each mother and father and daughter and son.   (Count four fingers.)

The Dreidel

Nun, gimmel, hay, shin.	(Count on four fingers.)
Put the nuts and candies in.	
Take a dreidel from the shelf,	
And let it spin and spin.	(Twirl finger.)
Nun means *nothing* if it shows.	(Make zero with thumb and finger.)
Gimmel is *one*, a number small.	(Hold up one finger.)
Hay means *half* of everything.	(Hit open palm of hand.)
But *shin* means win and take it all.	(Hold out two palms.)
Nun, gimmel, hay, shin.	
Spin the dreidel on the floor.	(Make spinning motion.)
Spin it like a spinning top,	
One and two and three and four.	(Show one finger at a time.)

(A dreidel can be made from a square of styrofoam or a section of an egg carton. Number the sides and let numerals stand for the Hebrew letters. Add a zero for nun. *Sharpen the end of a stick in the pencil sharpener and push it through the styrofoam to make a dreidel. Peanuts, raisins, or candy are divided equally among players. Everyone agrees on the number to be placed in a pile or dish. A child spins the dreidel or top, and if* nun *lands face up, the player gets nothing. No candy is put into the dish. If* gimmel *comes up, the player puts one candy into the dish. If* hay *lands face up, the player takes half of the candies. If* shin *shows, the player takes all of the candies.)*

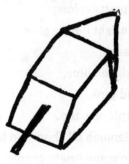

Hanukkah Is Here

One bright candle burning
Through the winter night.
Hanukkah is here,
Hanukkah is here.
Two bright candles burning,
A festival of light.
Hanukkah is here,
Hanukkah is here.

(Continue until eight candles are lighted. A mobile made of a wire coat hanger can be hung up; then stars of David covered with gold paper can be attached by string to the coat hanger.)

Hanukkah Lights

I want to be the one who lights
The candles which will brightly glow.
I'll light them all because we know
There is one candle for each night.
Each night of Hanukkah they'll shine,
1, 2, 3, 4, 5, 6, 7, 8, in a line.

(Use three tongue depressors or popsicle sticks and glue them to form a triangle. Sparkle them with glitter and put the triangles together to form a Star of David.)

Four Dreidels

The first little dreidel turns quickly around.   (Hold up one finger at a time.)

The second little dreidel makes a humming
sound.

The third little dreidel spins with a zoom.

The fourth little dreidel must have lots of room.

A dreidel, of course, is a four-sided top.

We spin it around with a hop and a stop.

A dreidel is friendly; a dreidel invites

Children to come to the Festival of Lights!

Hanukkah Candles

Eight little candles

Are standing in a row.

See their pretty colors.

See their bright flames glow.

Violet, orange,

Green, red, and blue,

Yellow and pink,

And a purple one, too.

See our Menorah all shiny and bright

Holding so many bright candles tonight!

*(Draw a Menorah shape on the chalkboard and
invite individuals to use colored chalk to complete the drawing with candles. Ask: "Can you
remember some rhyming words from the
poem?" row/glow; blue/too; bright/light.)*

Hanukkah Is Here Again

Hanukkah is here again.

We'll all receive some toys.   (Pretend arms are filled.)

Folks like the season very much,

Especially girls and boys.   (Point to self.)

The Menorah will give us lots of light.   (Wiggle fingers.)

We'll spin a dreidel, too.   (Spinning motion.)

We'll count the golden gelt we'll get   (Count fingers.)

So many things we'll do.

Five Little Spiders

Five little spiders on Christmas Eve

Wanted to see the pretty Christmas tree.

One said, "I'm afraid to go into the room."

Two said, "We're afraid of the mop and the broom."

Three said, "I hope someone won't step upon us."

Four said, "I hope that we won't cause a fuss."

Five said, "We just love pretty Christmas trees."

All said, "We hope that nobody sees."

So they crept through a hole in the wall that night,

And next morning, there was a wonderful sight.

For on Christmas Day all over the tree

Were the shiniest webs that you ever did see.

(Children volunteer to be spiders and memorize the verses in quotation marks. Ask someone to tell the "story" about the little spiders after you have read the poem once. Draw criss-crossed lines on the board to represent a web which children can copy. Make spiders from black pipe cleaners.)

A Counting Christmas Rhyme

Look under the tree! How many spacemen?

Count them with me. Five and five is _____.

How many presents are wrapped with fancy twine?

Count them with me. Five and four is _____.

How many hours do we all have to wait?

Count them with me. Four and four is _____.

How many ornaments are like the stars in heaven?

Count them with me. Five and two is _____.

How many jumping jacks are doing fancy tricks?

Count them with me. Three and three is _____.

How many teddy bears are looking so alive?

Count them with me. Three and two is _____.

How many mystery boxes can we explore?

Count them with me. Three and one is _____.

How many bicycles are there here to see?

Count them with me. Two and one is _____.

How many engines can really run for you?

Count them with me. There are only _____.

How many angels are on the Christmas tree?

_____ on top is all that I can see.

(Children supply the number each time. They hold up the correct number of fingers on each hand. This sophisticated counting rhyme can be used with second graders. Allow ample time for children to complete an addition problem. Write the addition statements on the board.)

This Baby Pig

This baby pig went to market.

This baby pig trimmed the tree.

This baby pig cooked the dinner;

And this baby pig brewed the tea.

This baby pig sang, "Merry Christmas!"

And he sang it on T.V.

(Bend down one finger at a time.)

Santa's Reindeer

One, two, three, four, five little reindeer.   (Point to one finger at a time.)

Stood by the North Pole gate.

"Hurry, Santa," called the reindeer,

"Or we will all be late!"

One, two, three, four, five little reindeer   (Point to fingers again.)

Santa said, "Please wait!

Wait for three more little reindeer,

Then we will have eight."   (Hold up three fingers on the other hand.)

(Ask the children to name the reindeer: Vixen, Comet, Cupid, Dancer, Dasher, Donner, Blitzen, and Prancer. Ask: "How many reindeer are there? What shall we do about Rudolph?")

Christmas Tree

Here is a great tall Christmas tree.   (Make large triangle shape with arms.)

That makes a pretty light.   (Wiggle fingers.)

Here are two little ornaments.   (Make two circles with thumbs and forefingers.)

On top is an angel bright.   (Point finger upward.)

Here are Santa's ten small elves   (Hold up ten fingers.)

That help in every way.

Here is Santa's jolly face.   (Make circle with fingers.)

And here is Santa's sleigh.   (Lock fingers and hold them downward.)

On Christmas Morning

At last, on Christmas morning,

What presents did we see?

A tractor for my brother,

A talking clown for me;

A string of pearls for Mother;

A sweater for my dad.

A red coat for my sister,

A machine that helps me add.

A teddy bear for Baby,

And for my pup a bone.

It was the nicest Christmas

That we have ever known!

(Ask the children to count the presents and tell how many there were altogether. Did anyone get more than one present? Who was it? Name another present each member of the family might have received.)

88

Three Little Pine Trees

Three little pine trees stood on a hill.	(Hold up three fingers.)
There was no wind; it was frosty and still.	(Fold hands.)
You would think they were statues so straight and so tall.	(Stand erect.)
Till the wind came roaring; for now it was fall.	(Move hands back and forth quickly.)
A cold, icy winter would soon arrive here.	(Hug body.)
In December, the oldest month of the year.	
The three little pine trees stretched up very high.	(Stretch body.)
And looked at the cloudy and dark snowy sky.	(Reach hands upward.)
Left and right, right and left they swayed side to side.	(Sway body back and forth.)
And furry small creatures all started to hide.	(Wiggle fingers and hide hand.)
Three little pine trees were covered with snow.	(Hands over head.)
And they silently knew that some day they would go.	
At last they were happy, for now don't you see	
Each is a beautiful tall Christmas tree.	(Wiggle fingers above head.)
Now three other pine trees stand on the hill.	
There is no wind, it is frosty and still.	(Fold hands.)

Three Fir Trees

Three fir trees grew on the mountain side.
Three little fir trees stood with pride.
The first tree had a furry guest.
A squirrel stayed safe inside her nest.
The second tree was bright with snow.
A chipmunk had no place to go.
The third tree fell and left to be
A decorated Christmas tree!

Ways of Saying "Happy Christmas"

God Jul - Swedish and Norwegian

Feliz Natal - Portuguese

Froehliche Weihnachten - German

Buone Feste Natalizie - Italian

Joyeux Noel - French

Feliz Navidad - Spanish

Bozego Narodzenia - Polish

Glaedelig Jul - Danish

A Mouse's Christmas

Down in the cellar one dark Christmas Eve,

A little mouse wondered what she would receive.

She wrote, "Dear old Santa,

You know how to please,

So won't you please bring me

A small slice of cheese?"

Down in the cellar that bright Christmas Day,

The mice knew that Santa had come in his sleigh.

Each little mouse knew how to say "Please."

For Santa had left more than one slice of cheese.

(Ask: "Why do you like the mouse that wrote to Santa? Why did Santa listen to her? Do you like the way the rhyme ended? Why? Have you ever written a letter to Santa? Tell about it.")

Santas

One Santa, two Santas, three Santas, four.

I have counted many, but there are several more.

One is Santa in a store hearing girls and boys

Telling of their wishes for presents and for toys.

Two is Santa on the page of a magazine.

Three is Santa on the face of every T.V. screen.

Four is Santa on the street with a little bell.

Oh, there are many Santas, more than you can tell.

Five is Grandpa Santa walking in the yard.

Six is Santa's picture on a Christmas card.

But there is just one Santa that I will never see.

He puts all of my presents beneath the Christmas tree!

(Ask, "Why are there so many Santas? Where have you seen them? Have you ever talked to a Santa? Where?")

Santa and His Reindeer

Old Santa's reindeer pranced in the snow.

Old Santa's reindeer were ready to go.

Old Santa's elves were packing the toys

That Santa would bring to the girls and the boys.

The first reindeer said, "We really should hurry."

The second reindeer said, "There is no need to worry."

The third reindeer said, "It is almost midnight."

The fourth reindeer said, "We really should take flight."

The fifth reindeer said, "We should be on our way."

The sixth reindeer said, "Before Christmas day."

The elves packed the sleigh and Santa came out.

He jumped in his sleigh and he gave a big shout!

He called to each reindeer, "It's time we should fly

Over the housetops and up in the sky!"

And so, girls and boys, that's the end of the rhyme.

Old Santa Claus is always on time.

Dear Santa

Christmas Eve has come.

Will I get a drum?

Or a top with a _____ (hum)?

Or some chewing _____ (gum)?

Or a cowboy _____ (hat)?

Or a baseball _____ (bat)?

Or a pup or a _____ (cat)?

Or a violin and _____ (bow)?

Or some skis for _____ (snow)?

(Children supply the rhyming word at the end of each line. Transpose the questions by asking,

"What would you use for snow? What would go with a violin? What sound would a top make?" Suggest that children who can write "send" a letter to Santa. Ask, "Which of the presents mentioned in the rhyme would you like?")

Christmas Secrets

I know so many secrets

Such secrets full of fun;

But if you hear my secrets,

Please don't tell anyone.   (Whisper.)

Here are some lights that twinkle,   (Wiggle fingers.)

Here is an ornament.   (Make circle with fingers.)

Here is a great big present   (Measure.)

From Grandpa it was sent.

And on the very tip-tip top,

An angel you can see.   (Point up.)

What is the secret? Can't you tell?

Why, it's a Christmas tree!   (Stand and raise arms high.)

Boxes under the Christmas Tree

Mysterious boxes are under the tree.

I hope that one of them will be for me.

There's a very tall box. Now just guess what is in it.   (Measure tallness with hands.)

I tried but I never could guess for a minute.

There's a rectangular box, not a very big size.   (Measure shape.)

But I'm sure that it holds a most special surprise.

There's a little square box that I wonder about.   (Measure squareness.)

It holds a nice present; of that there's no doubt.

There's a triangular box. Now what could that be?   (Pantomime shape.)

It is such a strange shape to be under a tree.

And now for the round box. The lid is round, too.   (Make circle.)

Shall I listen and shake it? Now what would you do?

Well, it is past midnight. The hour is late.

I'll go to bed and so I will just have to wait.

But all night I will dream of the boxes I see

Under our beautiful green Christmas tree.

(Suggest that the children draw two-dimensional shapes to represent boxes of different sizes. Ask, "Can you think of other shaped boxes that might hold presents? What would you put into a tall box? a long one? a short one? a round one? What kind of box would hold a ring for Mother? What kind of box would hold a tie for Father? What kind of box would be needed for a television set? a toy space ship? a sweater? a cowboy hat? candy? What would you pack inside a very tiny box?" Bring in different shaped boxes and discuss their surfaces or faces. "How many sides the same size has a rectangular box? a square box?" Read Christmas Is A Time of Giving *by Jean Walsh Anglund; Harcourt, Brace and World, New York, 1961.)*

Five Christmas Stockings

Five Christmas stockings were hanging in a row.   (Hold up five fingers.)

Waiting for Santa to fill them top to toe.

Number one said, "I am happy because   (Point one finger at a time.)

Soon I shall see dear old Santa Claus."

Number two said, "A patch you will find

Here on my toe, but Old Santa won't mind."

Number three said, "I am really quite small,

But I think I could hold a ring and a ball."

Number four said, "I hear on the roof

The prancing and pawing of each little hoof."

Number five said, "Be quiet! Be quick!

I think I can hear our good friend, Saint Nick."

Five Christmas stockings were hanging in a row

And old Santa filled them from top down to toe.

A Star

Coming downstairs, well, what do we see?

A star right on top of our bright Christmas tree.   (Point to top of tree.)

Count every point. How many are there?

1, 2, 3, 4, 5. Why, I declare!

1, 2, 3, 4, 5. Yes, there are

Five points upon our bright Christmas star!

(Children may trace around a star figure and label the points with numerals.)

TOYS

In every country of the world, children play with toys. Toys are universally important to the growth and development of children. Factories turn out thousands of toys for all interests and occasions. Schools are equipped with varieties of books and toys for all ages. Often children make toys of their own. We can agree that a use of toys is one of the foundations of learning in early years and can help in the teaching of mathematical and other important concepts. Toys are associated with Christmas, Santa Claus, and Hanukkah.

Yo-Yos

A yo-yo can be yellow,

Red or green or blue.

If you toss a yo-yo,

It will come back to you.

A yo-yo is a kind of top

Tied to some yarn or string,

And it spins swiftly up and down

With a humming and a zing.

(Yo-yos are not new at all. In fact, boys and girls hundreds of years ago in the far East played with them.)

Three Yo-Yos

Three pretty yo-yos are made for play,   (Make circle with fingers.)

And each has a string that we wind this way.   (Motion of winding.)

I'll toss this blue yo-yo far, far away.   (Motion of throwing.)

But the blue yo-yo will come back to stay.   (Clap.)

I'll toss this red yo-yo with a loud zing.   (Circle with fingers.)

I wind and I wind and I wind its string.   (Motion of winding.)

I'll toss this green yo-yo and have lots of fun.   (Repeat same motions.)

But although I toss it, back it will come.

Three pretty yo-yos are made for play,

Each has a string that we wind this way.   (Motion of winding.)

(Bring in some yo-yos so that individuals may have practice in playing with them.)

A Toy to Make

Fold a square of paper

Fold it then once more.

Now we have some triangles:

One, two, three, and four!

Cut the paper on the folds.

Fold the corners in.

Tack the pinwheel on a stick,

And now we can begin.

Blow, blow, blow the pinwheel.

Make it go around

When you blow your pinwheel

It makes a buzzing sound.

(Give each child a square of paper to fold twice, cut on the folds toward the center, bring the corners back to the middle, and tack to a dowel stick. Do not let the children do the tacking and be sure the tack is driven far enough in the stick so it will hold.)

Tops

Five little tops were spinning on the floor.

This red spinning top spun right out the door.

This blue spinning top made a fine humming sound.

And this yellow top whirled around and around.

This green spinning top sang a song as it hopped.

This orange top went "tick-tick" and stopped.

Now the five spinning tops have all spun away.

Let's choose five more spinning tops to play.

Toys

Toys, toys, toys,

For many girls and boys.

Some can talk,

Some can walk,

And some make lots of noise.

Toys, toys, toys,

For many girls and boys.

Puzzles, boots,

A horn that toots,

That every child enjoys.

Toys, toys, toys,

For many boys and girls

A silver bike,

Shoes for a hike,

A dancing doll with curls.

Toys, toys, toys,

For many boys and girls.

A music box,

Some skiing socks,

Or a wind-up toy that whirls.

(Ask: "Which toy would you like for your birthday or Christmas? Did we leave out any important toys? Which ones? Can you make up a rhyme about one or two of them? Show us with your hands a toy you would like without saying a word to describe it.")

(Five children stand and turn around twice. Each child holds a circle of colored paper.)

(One child spins around and leaves the group.)

(Encourage humming. Child leaves the group.)

(Child leaves group.)

(Child leaves group.)

(Child leaves group.)

(Choose five different children and repeat the activity.)

The Balloon Man on the Corner

Hear the balloon man on the corner cry,

"Balloons, balloons! Who will buy?

Balloons, balloons, balloons, balloons!

As bright and round as big full moons."

_____ bought a red balloon and it was very light.

The red balloon sailed far away and soon was out of sight.

_____ bought a yellow one on that windy day.

The yellow balloon lifted up and sailed a mile away.

_____ bought a blue balloon, and oh it was such fun!

The blue balloon sailed to the clouds and went up to the sun.

_____ bought an orange balloon as quickly as a sneeze!

The orange balloon sailed away over hills and trees.

_____ bought a green balloon, and oh my gracious me!

The green balloon sailed away and went far out to sea.

Six balloons were all gone now; the children were so sad!

The green balloon—it was the last. The only one they had.

But the balloon man on the corner went back into the store.

He said, "I have enough balloons. I'll give you all some more.

Balloons, balloons, balloons, balloons,

As bright and round as big full moons!"

(Substitute the names of children. Suggest that they trace around a round template and color balloons for the flannelboard. Construction paper will lie still if the board is slanted slightly backward. Add a strip of yarn to each ballon. Children can then take off balloons one at a time and tell how many remain. They may dramatize the poem.)

WINTER

In winter, snow swirls in a confetti-like motion, painting the countryside white within an hour. It strips the autumn trees of their remaining colored leaves and causes icycles to weep from the eaves of buildings.

The cold wind shrieks and finds cracks in buildings through which it can whistle. Animals are now in hibernation and their fur becomes thick to keep them warm. Branches dance against the windows and logs sputter yellow flames in fireplaces. We look out the window and see snow plows piling drifts to one side so that vehicles can move on their way.

Children in their snowsuits feel the sting of snow against their faces as they drag sleds to the tops of hills. In the evening, there may be walnuts to crack or popcorn balls to mold and chew.

The world is covered with quiet white as a column of smoke curls from chimneys as if to say, "Be still! The beautiful season will not last forever. Enjoy it while you may."

Happy New Year

On New Year's Day, on New Year's Day,
This is what I always say:
"Happy New Year, Daddy,   (Hold up pointer finger.)
Happy New Year, Mother,   (Hold up ring finger.)
Happy New Year, Sister,   (Hold up small finger.)
Happy New Year, Brother."   (Hold up thumb.)
On New Year's Day, on New Year's Day,
This is what I always say:
"HAPPY NEW YEAR!"

I Am the Wind

I toss the kites up in the sky,   (Sweep hand upward.)
And help the people's clothes to dry.

I send down leaves in golden showers,   (Raise arm, move fingers, and lower them.)
And make warm blankets for the flowers.   (One hand over other.)

And then again, the seeds I sow
Change little raindrops into snow.   (Raise hands, move fingers.)

I pile the snow in drifts at night,   (Raise hands high.)
Till all the world looks cold and white.

And when the setting sun is red,   (Make circle of arms.)
I quiet down and go to bed.   (Palms together beside face.)

I Am a Snowman

I am a snowman made of snow.	
I stand quite still at ten below.	(Stand tall.)
With a big potato for a nose,	(Point to nose.)
And worn out shoes to make my toes.	(Point to feet.)
I have two apples for my eyes,	(Point to eyes.)
And a woolen coat about this size.	(Measure.)
I have a muffler warm and red,	(Circle neck with hands.)
And a funny hat upon my head.	(Hands on top of head.)
The sun is coming out. Oh, dear!	(Make circle with arms.)
The sun is melting me, I fear.	(Begin to sink slowly to floor.)
Oh, my, I was so nice and round,	
Now I'm just a puddle on the ground!	(Curl up on floor.)

Snow Ladies

Ten little snow ladies stood in a line,

Until Mister Warm Sun started to shine.

Two ladies melted for they couldn't wait.

So when we counted, we saw only _____.

Two of them melted faster than "ticks."

So when we counted, we saw only _____.

Six little snow ladies stood in a line,

Until Mister Warm Sun started to shine.

Two of them melted as two did before,

So when we counted, we saw only _____.

Four little snow ladies looked so divine

Until Mister Warm Sun started to shine.

Two of them melted right down to each shoe.

So when we counted, we saw only _____.

Two little snow ladies started to fuss,

"Why does old Mister Sun have to shine upon us?

We were so happy and it was such fun!"

But when they were counted, we saw not a one.

Ten little snow ladies melted away.

We hope they will come back some cold winter day.

(The children supply the missing numbers each time. On a second or third reading they can say much of the rhyme with you. Make a circle of arms for the sun. This rhyme helps children learn to count by two's.)

Snowflakes

Snowflakes look like dainty lace.

I felt three soft upon my face.

I felt two on my chin and lip

I caught one on my finger tip.

(Ask the children to draw snowflakes. Ask, "How many sides does a snowflake have?")

Making Snowballs

Roll, roll, roll the snow	(Motion of rolling snow.)
Roll it round and round.	
Make a great big snowball	(Make circle with arms.)
And lay it on the ground.	(Motion of placing it on ground.)
Roll, roll, roll the snow	
Round and round and stop.	
Make a snowball middle-sized	(Make smaller circle with arms.)
And lay it on the top.	(Motion of laying it on first snowball.)
Roll, roll, roll the snow	
A smaller ball instead.	(Make smaller circle with arms.)
Lay it on the middle one,	(Motion of laying snowball on top.)
And you'll have a head!	
Get a hat without a crown	(Hands on top of head.)
And potato for a nose.	(Point to each body part.)
Get a scarf and get a broom,	
And old shoes for the toes.	
Now our happy snowman	
Is sitting on the ground.	
It's the best time we have had	
All the year around!	

(Read White Snow, Bright Snow *by Alvin Tresselt; Lathrop, Lee, and Shepard, New York, 1947.)*

Mittens

Mittens for the snow time	
When the world is white.	
Mittens for my two hands.	(Hold up two hands.)
Mittens left and right.	(Indicate left and right.)
Mittens with a thumb place,	(Indicate thumb.)
Mittens warm and snug.	
Mittens make me feel like	
A bug inside a rug!	(Hug body.)

(On a snowy day, gather children's mittens. Put one mitten in one box and its mate in the other. Ask children to find mates for their mittens. Additional activity: A child keeps his/her fingers together, thumb outstretched, and asks a friend to draw around both hands. Then children cut out their own mittens and decorate them. They may cut felt mittens for the flannelboard.)

99

Roll a Snowball

Roll the snowball over and over. (Twirl one hand over the other in rolling motion.)

Roll the snowball over the ground.

Roll the snowball over and over.

Roll the snowball and make it round.

Roll the snowball, one for the body.

Roll a snowball, one for the head.

Find a straw hat, a coat, and some trousers,

Find a bright scarf, green, yellow or red.

(Read All Ready for Winter *by Leone Adelson; David McKay, New York, 1952.)*

Snowflakes in Our Town

The clouds are dark and in our town,

The flakes of snow are falling down.

One, two, three—they're falling fast. (Hold up three fingers.)

Four, five, six—they'll never last. (Hold up six fingers.)

Seven, eight, nine—they are so cold. (Hold up nine fingers.)

Ten, eleven, twelve—all I can hold. (Hold up ten fingers; stop and hold up two more.)

But, oh, here comes the happy sun!

They're melting!—twelve, eleven, ten, nine, (Count backward.)

Eight, seven, six, five, four, three, two, one!

(Write numerals through twelve on the board. Ask one child to point to each numeral as the rhyme is said. Ask another to point to each numeral in reverse at the end of the rhyme.)

January Snow

Here comes the month of January.

We are excited and happy and merry. (Clap three times.)

From a big gray cloud in the dark, dark sky,

A crowd of snowflakes are starting to fly. (Hand raised, fingers lowered.)

And so what will we do when snow covers the ground?

Should we tiptoe around and not make a sound? (Children say "NO.")

Should we get into bed like an old sleepyhead? (NO.)

Should we dress in warm clothes and go out of doors? (YES.)

Shall we make a snowball and hit the brick wall? (YES.)

100

Shall we laugh? Shall we shout and roll all about? (YES.)

As we feel the wind blow, shall we pile up the snow? (YES.)

What shall we do with that big pile of snow,

When it reaches our window? Does anyone know? (Children respond.)

We will roll it and roll it and roll it and then

We will make two snow ladies and two fat snowmen! (Show two fingers on each hand.)

Yes! Two snow ladies and two fat snowmen!

(Read to the class The Self-Made Snowman *by Fernando Krahn; J.B. Lippincott Co., New York, 1974 and* The Snowman *by Raymond Briggs; Random House, New York, 1978. Beat suds from soap flakes and dot the mixture on windows and mirrors. It can be washed off easily. Actions may also be dramatized; rolling snow, throwing a snowball, and so on. More mature children can memorize the lines.)*

The Winter

The day is cloudy. The wind is bold. (Hug body.)

Dress up warmly; you mustn't get cold.

Put on your coat, button up tight. (Button coat.)

Put on your left boot, put on your right. (Show each foot.)

Put on your scarf; put on your cap, (Hands around neck and then top of head.)

Put on your mittens, and clap, clap, clap. (Clap.)

Go out of doors and play and play.

Come in again, and then we will say:

Take off your coat buttoned up tight. (Repeat the same motions as before.)

Take off your left boot, take off your right.

Take off your scarf, take off your cap.

Take off your mittens and have a short nap. (Hands clasped beside face.)

Popping Corn

In January, cold winds blow.

Let's make five snowballs out of snow. (Hold up five fingers.)

And next, we'll walk out to the barn.

Inside we'll shell four ears of corn. (Hold up four fingers.)

We'll put the popcorn in a cup,

And then we'll fill the popper up. (Cup hands.)

101

The wind is cold. Please shut the door!   (Clap.)
Let's not spill popcorn on the floor!
Now every year when winter calls,
We pop some corn for popcorn balls.   (Close hands to form ball.)

Warm Clothes

I have two red mittens   (Show hands.)
My snowsuit is white.
They keep me snug and warm   (Children say this.)
I have a brown jacket
That zips me up tight!   (Pretend to zip zipper.)
It keeps me snug and warm.   (Children say this.)
I have a green scarf   (Hands placed on neck.)
That comes up to my nose.   (Point to nose.)
It keeps me snug and warm.   (Children say this.)
I have two red boots.   (Point to feet.)
That cover my toes.
They keep me snug and warm.   (Children say this.)

Three Little Penguins

Three little penguins
Dressed in white and black   (Spread hands.)
Waddle, waddle forward   (Waddling motion as children take a few steps.)
And waddle right back.
Three little penguins in a funny pose.
They are wearing their evening clothes.
Their suits are black and their vests are white.
They waddle to the left and they waddle to the   (Waddle left and right.)
right.
They stand on the ice and they look very neat
As they waddle along on their little flat feet.

*(Ask: "Where might we see penguins? Where
have you seen one? How are penguins different
from other birds?" The children act out this
rhyme. Ask them to draw penguins.)*

Dear Little Tree

Dear little tree, what will you do
When winter winds start to blow
And all of your leaves fall to the earth
And your branches are filled with snow?

"I'll be a home for a little mouse,

Or a hole for a squirrel to hide.

And my trunk will make a very nice place

For a skunk to sleep inside."

(Ask, "How do trees help us? How do they help animals? Let's pretend we are asleep inside the tree trunk as I play a soft tune on the piano/music box.")

Five Fat Walruses

Five fat walruses were at the North Pole.	(Hold up five fingers.)
One climbed upon the ice and fell into a hole.	
Four fat walruses swam toward the ice.	(Hold up four fingers.)
One bumped an iceberg which wasn't very nice.	
Three fat walruses had whiskers on their faces	(Hold up three fingers.)
One got bored and went to sleep; he didn't like the places.	
Two fat walruses went to look for food.	(Hold up two fingers.)
One swam far, far away; he wasn't in the mood.	
One fat walrus was tired of the play.	(Hold up one finger.)
She flipped a good-by with her tail and then she swam away.	

FEBRUARY

We now have had enough of winter and it has lost its excitement. The wind blows colder and fire burns steadily in the fireplace. Icycles melt and February has arrived. This promises us that winter is in its final stages and spring is on the way. The sun sinks later in the evening and rises earlier in the morning. Birds are hungry, for seeds and berries are scarce. Squirrels look for buried nuts.

Abraham Lincoln's and George Washington's birthdays are celebrated. One great joy in the classroom is Valentine's Day. Children draw, color, and make valentines and give them to their friends. Valentines are not new. They were given hundreds of years ago. In the British Museum in London, one can see more than sixty original valentines. Millions of valentines are sold each year in this country.

The Valentine Shop

There is the nicest valentine shop.

Before I pass, I try to stop.

Inside the shop, I always see

Valentines for my family—

Brothers, sisters, aunts, and cousins,

Friends and classmates by the dozens—

A tiny one, a nickel buys.

A dime is for a bigger size.

A quarter for a much bigger size.

A dollar for the biggest size.

(Have a valentine box where children can drop in valentines for their friends. Children draw smallest to largest size for seriation purposes.)

I'll Send You One Valentine

I'll send you one valentine, that's what I'll do.

I'll send you one valentine, and maybe two!

I'll send you two valentines, wait and see.

I'll send you two valentines, and maybe three!

I'll send you three valentines from the best store.

I'll send you three valentines, and maybe more!

I'll send you four valentines, that's all I can do

But on each one,

I will write, "I love you!"

Valentines to Give Away

I have a lot of valentines.

I'll give them all away.

1, 2, 3, 4, 5, and 6

On a February day.

This one has red rosebuds.

This one, tiny hearts.

This one has some cupids,

This one, golden darts.

This one has a bit of lace,

This one, ribbons pink.

Who shall get these valentines?

Let me stop to think!

1, 2, 3, 4, 5, and 6,

Tell me what to do.

Valentines, valentines,

Which shall I give you?

(Parents often donate discarded valentines which can be used, or children may make their own with paper and scraps from the odds and ends box.)

Making Valentines

In February, what shall I do?

I'll make some valentines for you.

The first will have a cupid's face;

The second will be trimmed with lace.

The third will have some roses pink;

The fourth will have a verse in ink.

The fifth will have a ribbon bow;

The sixth will glisten like the snow.

The seventh will have some lines I drew;

The eighth, some flowers—just a few.

The ninth will have three little birds;

The tenth will have three little words:

    I LOVE YOU!

(The odds and ends box will contain materials to inspire creativity in making valentines. Read the poem a second time and ask the children which valentine they would like to make.)

Valentines from a Store

Valentines, valentines,

I brought them at a store.

I probably have a dozen,

And maybe I have more.

Valentine hearts that are shaped like tarts.

Valentines of red for a crown on your head.

Valentines green with verses between.

Valentines blue that say, "I like you."

Valentines yellow for a lucky fellow.

Valentines pies the color of eyes,

Valentine cakes—for goodness sakes!

That's enough. I'm going to stop right here,

And make up some valentine poems next year!

(Ask for rhyming words: fellow, head, between, *and* pies. *Suggest that children draw valentines on different colored construction paper and cut them out for the flannelboard. Perhaps someone can make up a valentine poem.)*

Five Groundhogs

The first groundhog digs a home in the fall,

And curls up all winter rolled up like a ball.

The second groundhog comes out of his lair.

On February second to get some fresh air.

The third groundhog looks up at the sun.

He then sees his shadow and goes on the run.

The fourth groundhog at his dark shadow peeks,

He goes into his deep home for six more weeks.

The fifth groundhog hopes that skies will be gray

So that he'll know that spring's on its way.

(Dramatize, or use as a finger play. Show a picture of a groundhog. Review ordinal numbers.)

Groundhog Day

February second
Is Groundhog Day.
Will he see his shadow?
And what will he say?
If he says, "More cold,"
If he says, "More snow,"
Then into his hole
He will surely go.

(Hold up two fingers.)

(Hands shading eyes.)

(Hug body.)
(Raise arms and let fingers wiggle as they fall.)

(Fist behind back.)

SPRING

Springtime

Oh, springtime is the time for me
  When I can swing and touch the sky,
    Or swim and splash in some cool stream,
    Or watch the swift clouds sailing by.

A striped snake crawls through the grass.
  A bluejay scolds me from a tree.
    A little skunk behind a bush
    Comes out to take a look at me.

My friend, the spider, spins a web.
  A frisky squirrel comes out to play.
    The sunbeams catch me as I run.
    Oh, I hope spring has come to stay!

The March Wind

This March wind rattles the windows and doors.   (Dramatize, or point to one finger at a time.)

This March wind whistles and blusters and roars!

This March wind seems angry and bends giant trees.

This March wind will scatter whatever it sees.

This March wind blows softly, a kind, gentle breeze.

Then I go to sleep nicely, as ever you please.   (Palms together beside head.)

(Read Gilberto and the Wind *by Marie Hall Ets; Viking Press, New York, 1963 and* I See the Wind *by Kazue Mezumura; Thomas Y. Crowell, New York, 1966.)*

April Rain

Dance, little raindrops   (Children tap lightly on a book or the desk.)

Tap with tiny feet.

The seeds will awaken   (Continue tapping.)

When they hear our beat.

Grow, little seeds

And see the cloudy sky.   (Children begin rising.)

Stretch, little roots   (Children stretch.)

You'll be a flower by and by.   (Cup hands above head.)

(Children may enjoy making up a tune for this rhyme.)

Little White Clouds

One little white cloud   (Hold up one finger.)

Played tag in the breeze.

Two little white clouds   (Hold up two fingers.)

Looked down at the trees.

Three little white clouds said,   (Hold up three fingers.)

"Hi!" to a plane.

Four little white clouds smiled   (Hold up four fingers.)

And greeted a train.

Five little white clouds   (Hold up five fingers.)

Turned to dark grey,

And begun to cry on the earth today.   (Raise fingers in air and lower them gently.)

(Read The Big Rain *by Francoise; Charles Scribner's Sons, New York, 1961. Ask, "What is nice about rain? How does it help us? What fun can you have in the rain? Draw a rainy day picture.")*

Four Little Raindrops

Four little raindrops sat upon a cloud.

The thunder roared; it was very loud.

The four little raindrops then began to fall;

They knew that spring had finally come to call.   (Arms raised, and fingers descend slowly.)

One little raindrop fell upon my shoe.

Down came another, and that made _____.

Another little raindrop fell upon my knee.

It met the others and that made _____.

Another little raindrop—Oh, there are many more.

Count the little raindrops and we will find

_____.

Four little raindrops fell from the sky.

But the big, warm, happy sun will lift them by and by.

(Use this rhyme to help explain the water cycle. Ask the children how they would act out this rhyme. They supply the number remaining each

time. Say, "You might want to cut out some raindrops and back them with flannel bits to use on the flannelboard. What color will you use for raindrops? How many raindrops do you want to use? Can you make up verses for more than four raindrops? What would five raindrops do? Six? Seven? I will write down your verses and we will say them. Tell what you like about the rain. How does the rain help the earth? Seeds? Flowers?" Read The Tiny Seed *by Eric Carle; Thomas Y. Crowell, New York, 1970.)*

Rainy Day

"Rumble, rumble, rumble," hear the thunder say.

"We will bring big storm clouds. You can't go out today."

One little raindrop was clear as morning dew.

Another raindrop joined her, and then there were two.   (Pop up one finger at a time.)

Two little raindrops danced so merrily,

Another splashed upon the earth, and then there were three.

Three little raindrops heard the thunder roar.

Another fell right down kerplop, and then there were four.

Four little raindrops kept the grass alive.

Another one tumbled down, and then there were five.

Rumble, rumble, rumble. The rain clouds have gone.   (Hands behind back.)

So now I can splash with my plastic boots on!   (Take big steps.)

Umbrellas

I put on my raincoat.   (Pretend to put on coat.)

I put on my hat.   (Put on hat.)

I put up my umbrella   (Fingertips touching over head.)

Just like that!

Umbrellas go up,

Umbrellas go down,   (Point up and down.)

When rain clouds are dark

All over the town.

One raindrop and two,   (Hold up one finger at a time.)

109

Two raindrops and three,

My up and down umbrella

Is up over me   (Fingertips touching over head.)

Four raindrops and five,   (Hold up one finger at a time.)

Six raindrops and seven,

Raindrops are tumbling   (Raise arms and let fingers fall slowly.)

Down from the heaven.

Drip, drip, drip, drip!

I am dry as can be,

My up and down umbrella

Is up over me   (Fingertips touching over head.)

(Suggest that children draw a rainy day picture with umbrellas.)

Spring is Here

Spring is here! Spring is here!   (Clap four times.)

Winter is gone and two flowers appear. (Hold up two fingers.)

Three little robins begin to sing.   (Hold up three fingers.)

Four bicycle bells begin to ring.   (Hold up four fingers.)

Five children come out and jump the rope. (Hold up five fingers.)

Spring is here now! I hope, I hope!

(Ask, "What else reminds us of spring? What games do you like to play out of doors in spring?")

The Rain Cloud

There's a rain cloud in the sky.   (Point to sky.)

Now it's drifting down.   (Raise arms, move fingers and lower them.)

Slowly, slowly raindrops fall   (Repeat motion.)

Covering the town.

Splish, Splosh, Splatter, Plop!

Raindrops splatter as they drop.

Go inside and don't get wet.

There are lots of splashes yet.

Get your slicker or your coat,   (Put on imaginary coat.)

Run and find your little boat.

Put on boots, put on cap.   (Continue motions.)

Zip yourself up with a snap!

Splash in puddles, slosh in rain.   (Move hands up and down.)

Watch the rain run down the drain.

Now, come play and sail your boat.   (Wave hand to one side.)

The rain has stopped, take off your coat.   (Remove garments.)

Take off your boots, take off your cap,

Zip off your jacket with a snap.

Now lie down for a cozy nap.   (Stretch out on floor).

(This is a good rhyme to use for a rainy-indoors game. Children enjoy pantomiming the taking off and putting on of clothing.)

Special Umbrellas

The first umbrella is red.

It keeps rain off my head.

The second umbrella is yellow

For a very lucky fellow.

The third umbrella is blue.

It is one that I drew.

The fourth umbrella is brown.

I will carry it to town.

The fith umbrella is green

Fit for a king or a queen!

(One finger at a time may be held up to review ordinals. Suggest that the children draw and color umbrellas as a rainy day activity. Read My Red Umbrella *by Robert Bright; William Morrow, New York, 1959 and* Umbrellas *by Taro Yashima; Viking Press, New York, 1958.)*

Umbrellas in Many Colors

Umbrellas help in many ways.

This black one is for rainy days.

In summer, when there's too much sun,

I carry this bright orange one.

This umbrella pink and neat

Fits at the table where I eat.

This red one when I put it up

Looks like an upside-down big cup.

(Ask the children to take out their crayons and hold up the correct color as you read the poem aloud. Suggest that they draw and color their favorite umbrella. Ask, "How many umbrellas are mentioned in the rhyme? Can you think of another use for an umbrella?" Ask them to say the rhyming words in the poem: days *and* ways, sun *and* one, neat *and* eat, *and* up *and* cup. *Read the poem again and ask the class to help you with the words.)*

111

My Spring Garden

Here is my little garden,	(Make bowl shape with hands.)
Some seeds I am going to sow.	(Motion of scattering seeds.)
Here is my rake to rake the ground.	(Scratch with fingers.)
Here is my handy hoe.	(Arms outstretched in front of body, bend fingers downward.)
Here is the big, round, yellow sun,	(Make circle with arms.)
The sun warms everything.	
Here are the rain clouds in the sky.	(Point to sky.)
The birds will start to sing.	(Move forefinger and thumb several times.)
Little plants will wake up soon,	(Stoop slowly and then rise.)
And lift their sleepy heads.	(Raise arms.)
Little plants will grow and grow	
From their warm earth beds.	

Ten Brown Seeds

Ten brown seeds lay in a straight row,
Said, "Now it is time for us to grow."
Up, up the first one shoots;
Up, up from its little seed roots.
Up, up the second one is seen;
Up, up, up in its little coat of green.
Up, up, up, the third one's head
Comes up, up, up from its little earth bed.
Up, up, up the fourth one goes;
Up, up, up—we can see its little nose!
Up, up, up the fifth one pops;
Up through the soil and then it stops.
Up, up, up the sixth we see;
Up it comes and it looks at me.
Up, up, up the seventh one peeps!
Up, up, up through the soil it leaps.

Up, up, up the eighth we spy;
Up, up, up to stretch to the sky.
Up, up, up the ninth one springs;
Up, up, up and everything sings.
Up, up, up the tenth grows fast;
Up, up, up and it is the last.
Up, up, up—the seeds every one
Become ten plants to smile at the sun.

(This rhyme demands fine body control. The children crouch down and one after the other rise slowly so that the growth does not take place before the couplet ends. On the last two lines, children stretch arms upward. Say, "Show how a seed looks when it is under the ground. You would curl up very small. Then slowly you would show one leg and arm at a time as you grow above the soil." Read Seeds Are Wonderful *by William Foster and Pearl Guerre; Melmont Publishers, Chicago, 1960.)*

Leaf Buds in March

Ten little leaf buds grew upon a tree.	(Hold up ten fingers.)
Curled up tightly as little buds should be.	(Make two fists.)
Now the little leaf buds are keeping snug and warm.	

112

All through the winter weather and the storm.

Along comes the cold and the windy month of March

His breath is icy and it is strong and harsh.

He swings the little leaf buds very roughly, so,

Then very, very gently he moves them to and fro.

Until the little raindrops fall down from the skies.

And the little leaf buds open up their eyes.

(Wave hands back and forth.)

(Swing arms back and forth vigorously.)
(Same arm movements, except slowly.)
(Raise arms and let moving fingers fall.)

(Make a fist and let one finger at a time pop out.)

Five May Baskets

Five May baskets are waiting by the door.

One will go to _____, and that will leave _____.

Four May baskets, they were made by me.

One will go to _____, and that will leave _____.

Three May baskets (I hope one is for you.)

One will go to _____, and that will leave just _____.

Two May baskets for children having fun.

One will go to _____, and that will leave just _____.

One May basket, it is sure to go

To my friend, _____, the nicest person that I know.

(Substitute names of children or people. The class or individuals supply the missing number.)

A May Basket

Up the steps,

One, two, three, four,

I will ring the bell on your front door.

I'll leave a May basket just for fun,

I'll turn around and I'll run, run, run!

(Most preschools and kindergartens have stairs which the children can climb as they act out this rhyme.)

In My Little Garden

In my little garden with a lovely view,

Sunflowers are smiling, one and two.

In my little garden by the apple tree,

Daffodils are dancing, one, two, three.

In my little garden by the kitchen door,

Roses now are blooming, one, two, three, four.

In my little garden by the winding drive,

Violets are growing, one, two, three, four, five.

(The children hold up a required number of fingers each time. Ask: "Which flower do you like best? Which one would you like to draw and color?" Ask for rhyming words: view, tree, door, drive. *All of the rhyming words should be number words. Ask: "Have we left out any pretty flowers? Which ones?" Try to show pictures of these flowers.)*

113

The Wind and the Kite

The first wind said, "I'll sail a kite."

The second wind said, "But not at night."

The third wind said, "When it is light."

The fourth wind said, "Just do it right."

The fifth wind said, "With all your might."

The first wind blew; the kite took flight,

And soon the kite was out of sight.

The first wind said, "I'll sail a kite,

But not at night.

When it is light,

I'll do it right,

With all my might!

If it takes flight,

I hope it won't

Go out of sight."

(Review of ordinals: first, second, third, and so on. Ask pupils to try to count the number of rhyming words ending with ight *as you say the poem for them. Ask them individually to name all the words they can remember that end with* ight. *Ask: "Can you make an ending to the rhyme and let the kite come back from out of sight?" Invite the class to say the rhyme with you.)*

Friendly Kites

The first little kite that was sailing by,

Said, "Hi" to a yellow butterfly.

The second little kite sailed over the zoo,

And it said, "Hi" to a kangaroo.

The third little kite that is number three,

Said "Hi" to a buzzing bumblebee.

The fourth little kite on a bright spring day

Said, "Hi" to a farmer pitching hay.

The fifth little kite that was flying free,

Said, "Hi" to a budding apple tree.

Swoosh! went the wind and they all took a dive:

1, 2, 3, 4, 5.

(Five children may be chosen for kites. Other children may play the butterfly, insects, or apple tree. They may make kite shapes of construction paper for the flannelboard and back them with flocked paper or bits of flannel. At the end of the rhyme, one child counts and removes the kites.)

Seven Kites in March

Here's a kite for Monday,

And one for Tuesday, too.

Here's a kite for Wednesday

(All day I think of you.)

Here's a kite for Thursday.

And Friday—see me throw it!

Here's a kite for Saturday.

(I like you and you know it.)

Here's a kite for Sunday.

(I like to hear you speak.)

I flew all seven kites today,

For each day in the week!

(The child learns the days of the week in succession as he/she points to a finger each time a kite is mentioned. Refer to the calendar on the wall and ask the class to repeat all seven days in the week. Bring in a kite, if possible, and ask the children to watch as you put it together.)

(Children return to their seats one at a time.)

Here Is a Kite

Here is a kite that flies so high
It almost touches the clouds in the sky.
Here is a kite that is having fun,
Trying to touch the warm, smiling sun.
Here is a kite with a fancy tail.
It twitches and turns—just watch it sail.
Here is a kite with a great long string
It likes to know that now it is spring.
Here are four kites for the winds that blow.
Let loose the kites and off they will go.

Fly, Little Bird

Fly, little bird. Go back to your tree.   (Motion of flying.)
That's where your baby birds ought to be.
The tree branches sway from side to side.   (Sway body back and forth.)
But your dear baby birds are safe inside.   (Close fists.)
Their nest is as snug as snug can be   (Cup hands.)
Away up in a tall apple tree.   (Point upward.)

Seven Plump Robins

Seven plump robins were hopping all around,
Picking up bread crumbs off of the ground.
Two saw a yellow cat up in a tree.
Two flew away, then there were three!
One heard a black cat say, "Mew, Mew,"
He flew away, then there were two.
One saw a striped cat sitting in the sun.
One saw a white cat and she began to run.
Now there are no robins hopping all around
Picking up bread crumbs off of the ground.

(Children may supply the number remaining or use as a finger play. Ask: "Why did the robins fly away?" Children sit on the rug or the floor and leave the set as the rhyme indicates. They volunteer to be cats and robins.)

Puddles

One puddle, two puddles
Made by the rain.
Three puddles, four puddles
Down in the lane.
Five puddles, six puddles
We can wade through.
Seven puddles, eight puddles
Quite muddy, too!
Nine puddles, ten puddles
Covering tiny roots
Eleven puddles, twelve puddles—
We all need our boots.

(Cut gray ovals from felt and give one to each of twelve children who in turn place the figures on the flannelboard as they say this counting rhyme with you. Listen for the final "z" sound at the end of puddles. *Twelve children volunteer and come to the set as their number is called.)*

The Peanut Pirate

I knew that something was very near,

Else why would those peanuts disappear?

I put out a handful quietly

For a squirrel that lives up in our tree.

A bluejay came and quick as a streak,

He grabbed one peanut in his beak.

And then he flew down to the ground,

And covered it with leaves he'd found.

Then back again the bluejay flew

And took a peanut number two.

The bluejay then flew 'round the tree,

And took a peanut number three.

The bluejay wanted more and more

Flew down for peanut number four.

The bluejay hadn't had his fill

With number five clamped in his bill.

He spied me with his beady eyes,

And scolded me with loud, harsh cries.

But I was happy now because

I knew who the peanut pirate was.

(Children may take turns dramatizing the story-rhyme with real peanuts, subtracting one peanut at a time from the set. Suggest that they take turns telling the story. Explain that bluejays take things to their nests. Their cry soulds like, "Thief, thief, thief!" Find a picture of a bluejay to show the class.)

Birds and Spring

I am a bird, all dressed in black.

I flew away, but now I've come back.

I am a bird, all dressed in blue.

I like to fly and I like to sing, too.

I am a bird, all dressed in green.

I am the smallest bird ever seen.

I am a bird, I am orange, you know.

Whenever I fly, you can see me glow.

Four birds fly and four birds sing.

They all seem to know that now it is spring.

(Find pictures of these birds in encyclopedias to show the children. The first line of each couplet can be memorized easily. Ask: "Which color rhymes with back? *With* too? *With* seen?" *Point out that there is no rhyming word for* orange. *Suggest holding up crayons to show the colors.)*

Mr. Sun

The sun came up one morning   (Make circle of arms.)

It saw one mountain high   (Reach arms high.)

It saw two clouds go sailing   (Move hands back and forth.)

Across the wide, blue sky.

It saw three rivers rippling,   (Move hand in wavy motion.)

And running to the sea.

It heard four blackbirds singing   (Hold up four fingers.)

Out in the maple tree.

It saw five children playing   (Hold up five fingers.)

That morning at their school.

It saw six trout go splashing   (Motion of swimming—hold up six fingers.)

Out in the forest pool

It saw seven flowers folding   (Hold up seven fingers.)

As sunset filled the sky   (Palms together.)

Eight stars were shining brightly   (Hold up eight fingers.)

The sun had said, "Good-by."   (Close eyes and fold hands.)

(Ask the children if they can remember what the sun saw. Discuss the events in the rhyme. As you read the rhyme a second time, pause for children to supply the rhyming words. Listen for the "s" sound in saw, and the ing ending. One child is the sun. Others are birds. Desks or tables are trees. The sun hides and comes up slowly. Birds awaken and fly around the room. Birds return to their nests to sleep. Duplicate for third graders to read. Ask: "What were the clouds doing? Where were the blackbirds singing? Where were the trout splashing?")

A Cherry Tree

I had a little cherry stone

I put it in the ground   (One finger of right hand planting seed in curled-up palm of other hand.)

And when next year I went to look,

A tiny stem I found.   (Index finger raised.)

The stem grew upward with its leaves,   (Finger moves upward.)

And soon became a tree   (Arms extended upward.)

One day I picked some cherries ripe,

And had them for my tea.

(Suggest that children draw and color a tree with cherries.)

Five Little Seeds

Five little seeds, five little seeds   (Hold up five fingers.)

Three will make flowers   (Hold up three fingers.)

And two will make weeds.   (Hold up two fingers.)

Under the leaves and under the snow,

Five little seeds are waiting to grow.   (Hold up five fingers.)

Out comes the sun,   (Make circle with arms.)

Down comes a shower.   (Raise arms and lower moving fingers.)

And up come the three pretty little pink flowers.   (Hold up three fingers.)

Out comes the sun   (Circle with arms.)

117

That every plant needs,

And up comes two funny, little, old weeds.   (Hold up two fingers.)

St. Patrick's Day

St. Patrick's Day is here, you see.

We'll pick some shamrocks, one, two, three.   (Hold up three fingers.)

We'll count the leaves and look them over,

And maybe find a four-leafed clover.   (Hold up four fingers.)

I'll sew green buttons on my vest.   (Point to chest.)

Green for St. Patrick is the best.

I'll wear a green hat, very high,   (Measure height.)

And dance a jig—at least I'll try.   (Shuffle feet.)

(Suggest that children draw a picture of a shamrock. Show them a picture. Ask: "Can you show us how you would dance a jig?")

EASTER

Easter heralds the beginning of spring. There is an Easter parade where people wear their new finery and march down the street. There are hot cross buns. There is the Easter lily with its pure-white petals, and last and most important for children, the egg coloring and the egg rolling which are traditional activities at the White House, first started by President Madison's wife, Dolley Madison. The egg hunt is exciting.

Easter Hunt

The Easter hunt has now begun.

Get your baskets! Let's have fun

Hurry up and don't be slow,

Because egg-hunting we must go.

Here is one. Here are two.

Here are three. Here are four.

I am sure that we'll find more.

Here are five. Here are six.

That bunny rabbit has some tricks!

Seven and eight. Is that all?

I see one there beside the wall.

That makes nine. Look by the pen.

I see another; that makes ten.

Hey-ho! Hey-ho! I would like to sing

About egg-hunting every spring!

(If children have learned the ellipse-shape, they can draw, color, and cut out Easter eggs, decorating them with sequins and buttons found in the odds and ends box. They may lay their eggs on a table and pick them up as the rhyme is said. Most of the counting portion of the rhyme can be recited with the teacher even on the first reading. Your browsing table should have copies of The Golden Egg Book *by Margaret Wise Brown; Western Publishing Company, New York, 1977 and* The Easter Egg Hunt *by Adriene Adams; Charles Scribner's Sons, New York, 1976.)*

Five Young Rabbits

L.B.S.

1. One young rab-bit joined the pa-rade.

She was best, she led the rest. She was not a-fraid.

(More verses on next page)

1. One young rabbit joined the parade.
   She was best, she led the rest.
   She was not afraid.

2. Two young rabbits dressed up so fine,
   Marched along and sang a song,
   Keeping perfect time.

3. Three young rabbits feeling very proud,
   Stepping high as they went by,
   Waving at the crowd.

4. Four young rabbits looking very grand,
   Pink and white, left and right,
   Marching with the band.

5. Five young rabbits, this is what they said,
   "Parades are fun, but when we're done
   We're glad to be in bed."

(The children take turns being rabbits, pantomiming the action as the class sings.)

Hop and Stop

The first little rabbit went hop, hop, hop.
I said to the first rabbit, "Stop, stop, stop!"
The second little rabbit went run, run, run.
I said to the second rabbit, "Fun, fun, fun!"
The third little rabbit went thump, thump, thump.
I said to the third rabbit, "Jump, jump, jump!"
The fourth little rabbit went sniff, sniff, snuff.
I said to the fourth rabbit, "That is enough!"
The fifth little rabbit went creep, creep, creep.
I said to the fifth rabbit, "It's time to sleep!"

(Since there is repetition of words, the children should be able to say the entire rhyme with you the second time.)

See the Easter Bunny

See the Easter bunny on top of the hill.   (Hold up two middle fingers for ears.)

Look at her hopping up and down.   (Move hand up and down, or children may hop on one foot.)

120

Look at her tail so fluffy and white (Make circle with fingers.)

Look at her ears so tall and brown. (Hold up two fingers again.)

Oh, oh! She hears the tiniest noise! (Hand back of ear.)

Her two little eyes are as dark as coal. (Point to eyes.)

Her whiskers tremble each side of her face. (Wiggle fingers.)

And she scuttles away down deep in a hole. (Hands behind back.)

(Ask "Why do you think the bunny was afraid? What made the noise?")

Hippety Hop

An Easter rabbit came hopping by,

Hippety-hop, hippety-hop.

He wiggled an ear and he winked one eye,

Hippety-hop, hippety-hop.

He hopped in the meadow, he hopped on the hill,

Hippety-hop, hippety-hop.

And as far as I know, he is hopping still,

Hippety-hop, hippety-hop.

(Children say refrain. Several children pretend to be rabbits and give four hops to accompany the refrain. Ask: "Who was Hippety-hop? Draw a picture of him.")

Bunny, Bunny

Bunny, white bunny

With ears so tall. (Place pointer fingers beside head.)

And your two pink eyes

And a mouth so small. (Make O with mouth.)

Wiggle goes one ear. (Wiggle one finger.)

Wiggle goes the other. (Wiggle other finger.)

Hop, hop, hop, hop

Home to your mother! (Hop away in four hops.)

I Had an Easter Bunny

I had an Easter bunny. (Hold up one finger.)

One day she ran away.

I looked for her by moonlight. (Hand shading eyes.)

I looked for her by day.

I found her in the meadow

With her babies 1, 2, 3.

So now I have four rabbit pets

To run and jump with me.

SUMMER

From June until September people flee from their daily schedules for Fourth of July picnics, for vacations in the mountains, or to the seashore. Summer has come calling to meadow and stream. Fields of grain are ripening to be ready for fall harvests. Robins are keeping in tune. Flowers bloom. The warm sunshine brings color to early roses. Bees hum lively buzzes. Squirrels race to gather nuts for winter, knowing that summer will fade. Mountain streams are visited by anglers fishing for trout.

The fragrance of June is here. Lazy breezes whisper. Children stand near lemonade stands and call, "Ten cents a glass!" This is a fun time when children can visit the zoo and see hoppity kangaroos, peacocks with fine feathers, freckled tigers, candy-striped zebras, and rubber-necked giraffes.

Summer is the time for vacations when children can see new places and they will long remember the cool sea breezes, week-end camping, back-packing, watermelon slices, strawberry shortcake, and finding a four-leaf clover.

Summer days are days to cherish.

Things that Grow

Here is my little garden bed.

Here is one tomato ripe and red.

Here are two great, long string beans.

Here are three bunches of spinach greens.

Here are four cucumbers on a vine.

This little garden is all mine.

Here are three squashes, two radishes too.

Here are six onions for a stew.

(Hold up designated number of fingers.)

(Hold up three fingers on one hand and two on the other.)

(Hold up three fingers on one hand and three on the other, or five and one.)

I cannot begin to name them all.

Some will be ready in the fall.

(Write 3+1=, 5+1=, and 3+2= statements on the board. Ask the children if they know which vegetables will be ready to dig up in the fall - potatoes, turnips. Ask, "What other vegetables are grown? What helps them grow?" - we weed them, water them; use a hoe to chop weeds.)

122

Our Vegetables

Many of our vegetables grow underneath the ground.

Some are small, some are large, some are long, or round.

The first one we call spinach, fresh, crisp, and green.

The second one is cabbage; the third one, a string bean.

The fourth is a tomato, juicy, round, and red.

The fifth one is a radish and I eat it with my bread.

The sixth one is a carrot, crunchy, sweet, and long.

The seventh is an onion, and oh, but it is strong!

The eighth one is a squash; we'll cook it in a pan.

The ninth one is an ear of corn (but not corn in a can).

The tenth is a potato to mash or fry or bake.

What a delicious vegetable feast we will surely make.

(Ask room helpers to look for vegetable pictures in magazines; cut them out and mount them on small squares of construction paper the same size. These can be backed with flocked paper or flannel so that they will adhere to the flannelboard. This rhyme can be used for a vitamin health lesson and a discussion of vegetable colors such as red tomato, brown potato, green lettuce or peas, and so on. Some children are not familiar with all fruits and vegetables. Bring in some of the least perishable ones. Pass them around for the children to feel and smell. Choose the ones you wish the children to taste and cut them in small sections. Ask a child to describe a vegetable with eyes closed.)

Summer Creatures

A little brown rabbit one summer day

Ran out of the burrow so she could play.

She found one cabbage that she could eat

She found two carrots and one red beet.

Out in the meadow, there were two holes;

And out of them ran two furry, soft moles.

Jam

There is apple jam for breakfast,

And blueberry jam for lunch.

There is cherry jam for dinner,

Jam is so good to munch.

There is grape jam for my pancakes,

And gooseberry jam for toast;

But orange marmalade on crackers

Is the one I like the most.

(Cover small jars with crepe paper representing the colors of jam. As the rhyme is said, children take turns in picking up the appropriate jar. Ask them to discuss their favorite jam. Listen for the "j" sound in the word jam.)

Peaches

One yellow peach is divided into two.

Two yellow peaches I will give to you.

Three yellow peaches, we will eat them by and by.

Four yellow peaches will make a good peach pie.

Five yellow peaches—let's put them in a sack

And take them to school for an afternoon snack!

(Use as a finger play, holding up a finger on each hand to represent one, then two, three fingers, and so on. Listen for the "z" sound at the end of the word peaches.

(Hold up appropriate number of fingers to simulate number of vegetables.)

(Hold up two fists.)

(Hold up two fingers.)

123

At the foot of the tree sat one little toad,

And the rabbit chased the toad all the way down the long road.

Two squirrels sat up on the limb of a tree,

And there were two more I could hardly see.

Five field mice peeped out of their cozy small nest.

And then they ran out and joined all the rest.

They all played a game of hide and go seek

They all hid their eyes and they never did peek.

"What's that?" said the rabbit, "Out in the park.

It must be a dog. I can hear a dog bark."

The five little field mice crept into their holes.

The four squirrels ran off

And so did two moles.

The rabbit ran off

And the little brown toad

Was the only one left by the side of the road.

(Rather than use as a finger play, ask children to play the characters as you read the poem. Use for programming.)

(Hold up one finger.)
(Move hand quickly to the right.)

(Hold up two fingers on each hand.)
(Five fingers.)

(Hands over eyes.)

(Hold up five fingers, then make a fist.)
(Hold up four fingers and then make fist.)
(Hold up two fingers and then fist.)
(Show two fingers for ears and then hide them behind back.)
(Hold up one finger.)

The Merry-Go-Round

The merry-go-round is starting to go.

It won't wait for us, so come on! Let's go!

Hurry and climb on the merry-go-round

That circles and circles around and around!

Toot! Toot!

"So many bright horses go round and around and around.

And around on the merry-go-round!"

The first has a saddle as blue as the sky.

She tosses her head as she goes prancing by.

The second is purple, the third horse is red.

The fourth horse has gorgeous green eyes in her head.

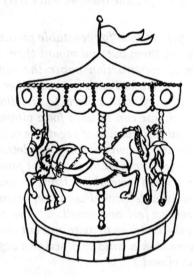

(Class says these lines.)

(One child stands and moves up and down.)

(Two children stand.)
(A fourth child stands.)

124

"So many bright horses go round and around and around.

And around on the merry-go-round!"

The fifth horse is brown with a fine, yellow mane.

He might try to buck! You should hold a tight rein!

The lavender horse is the sixth horse in line.

The seventh is black! Just look at her shine.

"So many bright horses go round and around and around.

And around on the merry-go-round!"

The eighth horse is green with a long flowing tail.

The ninth horse is orange—just look at her sail!

The tenth horse is pink with big dots all around.

Which one shall I ride on the merry-go-round?

"So many bright horses go round and around and around.

And around on the merry-go-round!"

The music gets slower and slower and then

We stop, but we all want to ride once again.

1, 2, 3, 4, 5, 6, 7, 8, 9, 10

I'll ride any time so just tell me when!

(Read the poem aloud. Ask: "Which horse do you want to ride?" Tie a colored piece of crepe paper around the wrist of the child who is to ride a certain colored horse. If the children can ride stick horses, how grand! Otherwise, they will ride "pretend" ones as they imitate horses going up and down on the merry-go-round and form a large circle of ten. Have a merry-go-round attendant ask: "Who rides the first horse? Who has number one horse?" The child answers: "I have the first horse." The attendant may sell tickets to ten more children who choose their horses. Read The Little Carousel *by Marcia Brown; Charles Scribner's Sons, New York, 1946.)*

(Children repeat two lines.)

(A fifth child stands, and so on, until all ten are standing and moving.)

(Class says these lines.)

(Class says these two lines.)

(Class counts participants.)

SEASHORE

The Seashore

Summer is a fine time to visit the beaches,
To eat pink ice cream cones, ripe berries, and peaches.
Summer is a time to decide what to do.
Shall we go to the seashore, the circus, or zoo?
Now won't you tell me just what YOU would do?
A seashore in summer is glorious fun.
Come with me now, and enjoy all the sun!

A Seashell

One day, a little shell washed up	(Hold shell.)
Out of the waves at sea.	
I held the shell up to my ear,	(Hold shell to ear.)
And I heard it sing to me.	
Sh--- sh--- sh--- sh!	(Children repeat.)
A little shell washed up one day,	
And lay upon the sand.	(Hold shell in hand.)
It sang a song about the sea,	
As I held it in my hand.	
Sh--- sh--- sh--- sh!	(Children repeat.)

(This is excellent for practice on the "sh" speech sound. Bring in a conch shell and let children one at a time hold it to the ear to hear the sound of the sea.)

Here Is a Starfish

Here is a starfish;	(Place one hand on table, fingers spread apart.)
Here is a shell.	(Show palm, hand slightly cupped.)
Here is an octopus;	(Place two palms together, fingers extended.)
Here is a bell.	(Lock fingers with one another; point down.)
Here is a fishnet;	(Interlace fingers.)
Here is a fish.	(Make swimming motions.)
Here is a birdbath;	(Two hands cupped.)
And here is a dish.	(One hand cupped.)

-Olive Amundson

126

Ten White Seagulls

Ten white seagulls	(Hold up ten fingers.)
Just see them fly	(Motion of flying.)
Over the mountain,	
And up to the sky,	(Raise arms high.)
Ten white seagulls	(Repeat motion.)
Crying aloud,	
Spread out their wings,	
And fly over a cloud.	(Motion of flying.)
Ten white seagulls	(Repeat motion.)
On a bright day.	
Pretty white seagulls,	
Fly, fly away!	(A small group "fly" around the room.)

Octopus, Octopus

Octopus, octopus down in the sea,	
How many arms can you show to me?	
Only one, or will it be two?	(Show one finger, then two.)
Why are all of these arms on you?	
Will it be three or will it be four?	(Show three, then four fingers.)
Oh, dear me! Are there really more?	
Will it be five or will it be six?	(Show five, then six fingers.)
I think that my eyes are playing tricks.	
Will it be seven or will it be eight?	(Show seven, then eight fingers.)
Tell me, octopus. I cannot wait.	
Octopus, octopus, down in the sea,	
How many arms can you show me?	
Child: "I have eight arms, as you can see."	(Show eight fingers.)

(Draw a circle for the body and add eight arms. Paint a paper sack gray and stuff it with newspaper, tie it at the neck. Then add eight crepe paper strips for arms.)

Going to the Seashore

I go to the seashore	
In the warm sand.	
I go walking with ten toes,	(Hold up ten fingers.)
And oh, it feels grand.	
I build a large castle	
In the warm sand.	
I shape it higher than my head	(Measure height.)
With my own two hands.	(Hold up hands.)

Five Big Waves

I went to visit the beach one day,

And I saw five waves begin to play.

The first wave gave a great big swish!

The second wave washed up several fish.

The third wave washed away my boat,

And there I saw it was afloat.

The fourth wave washed away a shell.

The fifth wave made a little swell.

The five waves played with me all day,

And suddenly, they went away.

(Draw five waves on the board and number them left to right. Children move left to right each time the word "washed" is said. Children will learn that first, second, and third are the same as one, two, and three. Ask them to continue the rhyme and tell what the sixth, seventh, and other waves did. Write the responses.)

Seashore Fun

What will I take to the seashore today?

What will I take and what will I play?

I'll take one shovel, I'll take one pail.   (Hold up pointer fingers on each hand.)

I'll make two red paper boats to sail.   (Two fingers on each hand.)

I'll watch three ships on the purple sea,   (Hold up three fingers.)

And I'll take four friends to play with me.   (Hold up four fingers.)

(After reading the rhyme, ask individuals if they can remember how many ships, friends, shovels, pails, and paper boats were mentioned. If not, read the rhyme again so that children can have a short period of learning to concentrate. Ask: "Have you been to the seashore? Tell about your experiences. Did you do any of the things the poem told about?")

FOURTH OF JULY

Our Flag

As red as a fire,
As blue as the sky,
As white as the snow—
See our flag fly!
Three pretty colors
Wave at the sky,
Red, white, and blue
On the Fourth of July!
Red, white and blue
Those colors are,
And every state has its very own star.
Hold up the flag
Hold it up high,
And then say, "Hurrah,
For the Fourth of July!"

(Discuss states in the union. Which are the newest states?-Hawaii and Alaska. Ask: "How many stars are there? What do the stars stand for? Can you draw a flag?")

Stars and Stripes

Red, white, and blue   (Hold up three fingers.)
Red, white and blue
Red means brave,
White means pure,
The color blue means true.
Red, white and blue,
Red, white, and blue.
Fifty stars for states we know   (Write "50" on the board.)
In our flag, row by row,
Some of the stars are new.
Red, white, and blue,
Red, white, and blue,
Thirteen stripes of red and white   (Write "13" on the board.)
Six and seven left and right,
They make a lovely view.

(Bring in a small flag for discussion. Count the rows of stars, and the stars in each row. Count the stripes, white and red separately. Explain that thirteen *means the first thirteen states in the Union. Discuss flag etiquette: Never let it touch the ground. Never let it touch anything below the ground, the floor, or water. Never use it as a costume or trim anything with it. Never carry it upside down. Never display it in the rain. Never write or draw on it. Always carry it high in the air and remember that it is a symbol of our country. Ask: "How many names of states can you remember? What is the name of our state? Have you lived in another state? Where? Do you have relatives in other states? Where?")*

Salute the Flag

Four children take a walk today.	(Hold up four fingers.)
They see a pole with a flag on top.	(Point upward.)
The flag is red and white and blue—	
And when they see the flag, they stop.	
They say "I *pledge*" or *promise.*	(Hand over heart.)
Allegiance is *loyalty.*	(Children echo each line after you.)
Republic means our *government.*	
One *nation,* under God, will be.	
Indivisible, not *divided,*	
And *liberty* means *free.*	
Justice for all means *fairness.*	
For all means *you* and *me.*	

(Discuss further meaning of the unfamiliar words such as justice, allegiance, pledge, *and re-public. Say* The Pledge of Allegiance.*)*

The Fourth of July Parade

We are having a Fourth of July parade,
A parade on the Fourth of July!
Sammy proudly carries the flag,
Straight, and tall, and high.
Sally plays a triangle, ding!
Billy tootles a flute.
Beth bangs two lids with a clang!
And Jack wears a sailor suit.
Elizabeth loudly blows a horn.
Jimmy whistles a tune.
Mary hits a frying pan
With a big, long iron spoon.
Hooray, hooray for the Fourth of July!
For the Fourth of July, hooray!
We will march along and sing a song
For the good old U.S.A.

(Select eight children to dramatize the rhyme. Use a triangle, flute, lids, horns, frying pan, and spoon for a "real" Fourth of July band. Substitute names of children in the class.)

BIRTHDAYS

Birthdays are always occasions to celebrate. The teacher usually is sure that each child who has a birthday during the school year is given recognition. Often, parents will bake cakes or cookies and prepare lemonade so that each celebration of a birthday can be shared with others.

Famous birthdays can be discussed. George Washington, as father of our country, cared for our country when it was new, just as a father cares for his children. Along with other presidents, he worked hard to help build a fine, strong government.

Lincoln's birthday is another holiday that should be noted. Abraham Lincoln's patience was torn when the country was at war. His birthday should be remembered. Children will learn of Lincoln's belief in freedom for all. Martin Luther King's birthday is of consequence, for he too believed in freedom and equality.

Mother's and Father's birthdays can be observed by suggesting that the children make birthday cards or gifts such as tracing handprints, putting together a small scrapbook of drawings, or designing a birthday card with a verse inside.

The Birthday Child

A birthday child had a birthday cake

With five candles burning bright.   (Hold up five fingers.)

She blew out two of the candles,

How many still had light?   (Hold up three fingers.)

How old is the birthday child? Do you know?

She is five years old. She told me so!   (Hold up five fingers.)

(Change the word five *to* six *if used in the first grade.)*

Four or Five Candles

Two candles,   (Hold up two fingers on left hand.)

Two candles,   (Hold up two fingers on right hand.)

That makes four.

I cannot see any more.

Four pretty candles, all the same—

Blow them out to play this game!

One (blow), two (blow), three (blow), and four (blow).   (Blow on fingers as if blowing out candles.)

Are they all gone? Are there more?

Oh, yes, I see another one.   (Hold up one finger.)

That makes five for birthday fun!   (Hold up five fingers.)

Five pretty candles, all the same—

Blow them out to play this game!

One (blow), two (blow), three (blow), four (blow), five (blow)!

For goodness sake!

Now please cut the birthday cake.

(Hang a calendar on the wall where you have marked the child's birthday. Birthdays are special and should be made meaningful. Ask children to choose a special birthday song. Optional verse: "The candle lights are playing tricks. Here's another! That makes six.")

Animal Birthdays

Animals have birthdays,

Of course they do!

Farm animals, pets,

Or those in a zoo,

How old is your gerbil?

How old is your dog?

How old is your cat,

How old is your frog?

How old is your pony?

How old is your hen?

Or duck, goose, or rabbit

That lives in a pen?

Did I mention your pet,

Or did I forget?

(Ask individuals to discuss the age of their pets. Say, "If you do not know, find out and tell us tomorrow. How do you take care of your pet? What kind of birthday present could you give your pet?")

(Blow on fingers as if blowing out candles.)

Happy Birthday

I had one candle on my cake,

When I was one, so I've been told.

I had two candles on my cake

Because then I was two years old.

I had three candles on my cake.

They said that I could have no more.

The next year, on my birthday cake,

I had four candles. I was four.

Now I am one year older.

I'm five years old—best age to be.

I have five candles on my cake.

Please sing a birthday song to me!

Alternate verse:

Now I am two years older and

I'm six years old—best age to be.

I have six candles on my cake.

Please sing a birthday song to me!

(Hold up one finger, then two, and so on, to represent the ages. Use for special occasions when a child in the room has a birthday. Listen for the "z" sound at the end of the word candles. *Ask, "Who has a birthday this week? Show us on the calendar. Next month? Show us the date and month of your birthday." Cover a small round hatbox with crepe paper and use for a birthday cake. Glue on candle holders for candles.)*

February Valentines

The calendar says it's February,   (Point to month.)

The second month this year.   (Hold up two fingers.)

And I know there's something

We all would like to hear.

_____ has a birthday;   (Substitute child's name.)

He's/she's _____ years old today.   (Children supply number.)

Perhaps there's something we can do,

Or something we can say,   (Ask the children what they might do or say on _____'s birthday.)

I have something for us,

So open up your eyes.

Here is a lovely birthday cake,

A Valentine surprise!   (If not used for Valentine's Day, substitute "wonderful.")

(Ask the class who should put the candles in the candle holders. Who should blow them out? Perhaps a parent will bake a cake for the occasion.)

Three Bright Quarters

Here are three bright quarters.

This one is for gum.

This one's for a popsicle.

This one's for my chum.

And it will stay here in my purse

Until her birthday comes.

(Make circle with fingers for quarters. Point to one finger at a time. Suggest that children make up their own story on what to do with their own quarters. Rhyming words are immaterial.)

Song about Birthdays

(Tune: *The Farmer in the Dell*)

We clap and clap and clap,

We clap and clap and clap.

We are five years old this year.

We clap and clap and clap.

Birthdays are such fun.

Oh, birthdays are such fun!

We are five (six) years old this year

Oh, birthdays are such fun.

In another year,

Yes, in another year,

We will all be six (seven) years old

Birthdays are such fun!

(If all children are five or six years old, the entire group sings. If one child in the class has a birthday that day, sing: "You are six years old today." Listen for the th quiet sound in the word birthday. Suggest that children make special birthday hats to wear by folding paper to points that will fit heads.)

133

Ready for Your Birthday

Who has a birthday?

Who has a birthday?

Who has a birthday?

Will you please stand?

Is it tomorrow?

Is it tomorrow?

Is it today?

Please hold up your hand.

Hold up your fingers,

Hold up your fingers,

Hold up your fingers,

That tell me your age.

Give me the number,

Give me the number,

Tell me how many

To write on this page.

(Write on a large sheet of paper with felt-tip pen, "Eddie" - or other name - "is six years old today." Write the numeral on the chalkboard. Ask the class what they would like to do to celebrate Eddie's birthday. Discuss the concepts of yesterday, tomorrow, and today in relation to time. Use a calendar for this purpose. Say: "Yesterday was the seventh of April. Tomorrow will be the ninth of April. Today is the eighth of April, Eddie's birthday!")

Conversations about a Birthday

Birthdays are mirthdays and worth special times.

_____ has a birthday, so let's make up rhymes.

Think of things that are new and good things to do.

Do you want to wind up a string?

(Children respond by saying, "I don't want to wind up a string.")

Do you want to sing about a king?

(Negative response.)

Do you want to draw a large ring?

(Negative response.)

These are not good things to do on a birthday.

Do you want to sit on the ground?

(Negative response.)

Do you want to hammer and pound?

(Negative response.)

Do you want to turn things around?

(Negative response.)

These are not good things to do on a birthday.

Then what good things shall we do?

Shall we take out some crayons?

Shall we draw? Shall we make

A fine birthday card or a nice birthday cake?

(Children respond affirmatively.)

_____ is six years old today.

Let us all clap and let's shout HOORAY!

(Children respond.)

A card or a cake? Which one will you make?

(Response.)

(This selection is neither a finger play nor an action rhyme, but rather one which stimulates conversation followed by the action of painting, coloring, or drawing as well as the action of speaking. The children make their cards or drawings of cakes, sign them, and give them to the child who has a birthday.)

Baking a Birthday Cake

Mix the cake-mix quickly.

Add an egg or two.

Then some water. Can you guess

What I will bake for you?

Add some sweet vanilla,

A small teaspoon will do.

Now put the mixture in a pan.

Do you have a clue?

Take it from the oven,

And let it cool awhile.

Spread pink frosting on it.

Does that make you smile?

Now to get some candles,

Yellow, white, or blue.

Count the candles. Put them on

A birthday cake for YOU!

(Bring in an electric oven so that children can watch the cake bake and time it. Use cake mix, water, and an egg or two. Let the "birthday" child help spread frosting and put on the candles. Include as many children as possible in the process: stirring, breaking eggs, adding water, vanilla, and so on. Ask volunteers to describe what was done or tell the story about baking a birthday cake. Ask: "How many candles will you have on your cake this year? Next year?" Read The Giant's Birthday *by Janet McNeill; Henry Z. Walsh, Inc., New York, 1961.)*

Birthday for Piglets

This baby pig had a birthday.

This baby pig fixed the lunch.

This baby pig baked the cupcakes,

And this baby pig mixed the punch.

This baby pig—well what did she do?

She sang, "Happy birthday!

Happy birthday to YOU!"

(From a pig pattern, children may trace, color, and back figures for the flannelboard; or the selection can be used as a finger play.)

135

THE CIRCUS AND THE ZOO

The circus and the zoo can provide the setting for recreational excursions. No audio-visual device can produce the thrills of the combined sights, sounds, and smells of a circus or zoo.

At a circus, there are daring feats of acrobatic skill, the antics of clowns, and the performance of animals.

The zoo is especially valuable when the visit is made at an impressionable age. Young children will observe the differences in sizes of animals, and note their eating, sleeping, and playing habits. The exact colorings are a wonder to the child.

After a visit to the circus or zoo, a flood of communication will be encouraged by the teacher and increased learning will take place. Those trips will provide many opportunities to sing, say poems about, dramatize, and discuss the experience.

Children will enjoy selecting scarves, necklaces, and hats from the dress-up or odds and ends box to make costumes for a circus parade. Paper bags worn over heads will lend realistic touches to the event.

Five Big Elephants

Five big elephants—oh, what a sight,

Swinging their trunks from left to right!

(Crouch over and clasp hands. Move arms left and right as the walk continues around the room.)

Four are followers, and one is the king.

But they all walk around in the circus ring.

(Choose four children to be elephants who follow one chosen to be king. They walk around the room several times as the rhyme is recited.)

-Traditional

(Choose five children; then five more until each child is in the ring.)

Big Gray Elephant

The big gray elephant slowly walks.

She doesn't make a sound.

(Children take giant quiet steps.)

She swings her trunk from left to right

(Stoop and lower arm; move back and forth.)

When she puts her feet on the ground.

Swing, swing, left and right,

She doesn't make a sound.

(Read Elephant in a Well *by Marie Hall Ets; Viking Press, New York, 1972.)*

Tiger Walk

Walk, walk, softly—slow—
This is the way the tigers go.
Walk, walk, get out of the way!
Tigers are coming to school today.
Creep, creep—softly—slow—
This is the way the tigers go.
Creep, creep, come and play.
Tigers are here at school today.

                              -Traditional

*(Children take slow measured steps throughout
the rhyme. Repetitive words will be easy for children to memorize.)*

The Menagerie

One big rhinoceros
Yawns politely with no fuss.
Y—awn! Y—awn!   (Children yawn.)
Two gray elephants
Do a very dainty dance.
Brrr-ump! Brrr-ump!   (Slap palms on desk.)
Three little tiger cats
Are waiting for some friendly pats.
Pat, pat, pat!   (Pat chest.)
Four little crocodiles—
We like their wide and happy smiles.
Aaaa-p! Aaaa-p!   (Snap fingers like jaws.)
Five lively kangaroos
Are breaking in five pairs of shoes.
Thump, thump, thump!   (Fists against palm.)

                    -Olive Amundson

Get-Together

A whooping crane came walking,   (Keep legs straight and walk tall.)
He wanted to have fun.
But he was very lonesome,
For he was only one.
The whooping crane kept walking,
Till he came to the zoo,

And there he met a camel   (Hunch over back and walk.)
And he, of course, made two.
The camel and the whooping crane,
They stood beneath a tree.
A huge baboon then came along,
And he, of course, made three.
They talked about the friendly zoo.
They heard an awful roar.
A lion with a yellow mane
Came by and there were four.
A great big lumbering animal
Was next one to arrive.
She said, "I am an elephant,"   (Lean over and swing arms for trunk.)
And she, of course, made five.
Next was a monkey-doodle
All full of funny tricks.   (Jump up and down.)
He said to them, "Why, howdy-do,"   (Tip imaginary hat.)
And he, of course, made six.
And then there came the tall giraffe,
Her neck stretched up to heaven.
She bowed and smiled at everyone,
So she, of course, made seven.
A polar bear came lumbering by.   (Walk awkwardly.)
She said, "I'm very late.
If I can stay and play with you,
Of course, we will be eight."
A great huge hippopotamus   (Arms curled at sides of simulate bulk.)
Thought it was time to dine.
He stayed and ate a bale of hay,
And he, of course, made nine.
A moose with antlers on his head   (Spread fingers on each side of head.)
Was kept inside a pen,
But he got loose, the daring moose,
And he, of course, made ten.
The animals all danced around   (Ten children march around room.)
They played some zoo games, too.
They were so happy they were friends,
And had their own fine zoo.

138

(Say, "Let's play zoo. Who will be the hippopotamus? the elephant? the giraffe? the moose? I will give each of you a card with your name on it. A visitor will come to the zoo and ask, 'Which animal are you?' You might answer, 'I am a lion.' The visitor may say, 'I am looking for an animal with a long trunk.' The elephant steps forward and says, 'I am an elephant. I have a long trunk.' We can have a lot of conversation with visitors today." If children can read, duplicate the poem for each child. Children not acting out the rhyme indicate numbers on fingers.)

Rhinoceros

A rhinceros, a rhinoceros

Sometimes he makes a dreadful fuss.

He has a big horn on his nose.   (Extend pointer finger from nose.)

He snorts and rumbles as he goes.   (Children say, "Grrrump!")

He's very long and very wide.   (Measure length and width with hands.)

He has a very wrinkled hide.   (Wavy motion with hands.)

He has big hoofs on his four feet.   (Hold up four fingers.)

We feed him grass and hay to eat.

A rhinoceros, a rhinoceros

Is surely not a pet for us.   (Shake head negatively.)

(Show a picture of a rhinoceros. The rhyme may be written on a wall chart. Ask, "Why wouldn't a rhinoceros make a good pet?")

Circus Time

First child: We will see a big parade.

All: The circus is coming to town.

Second child: We'll have pink lemonade.

All: The circus is coming to town.

Third child: The horses will put on a show.

All: The circus is coming to town.

Fourth child: The clowns will march in a row.

All: The circus is coming to town.

Fifth child: There will be some acrobats.

All: The circus is coming to town.

Sixth child: There will be some tiger cats.

All: The circus is coming to town.

Seventh child: There will be a buffalo.

All: The circus is coming to town.

Eighth child: Come on! Let's go! Let's go!

All: The circus is coming to town.

(Eight children will each have a line to say. The rest of the group says the refrain: "The circus is coming to town." Ask the eight children to choose eight more friends until everyone who wishes may have a turn saying one of the lines. On the last line, they march once around the room.)

139

This Funny Clown

This funny clown is round and fat.

This funny clown wears a silly hat.

This funny clown is tall and strong.

This funny clown sings a Western song.

This funny clown is very small,

But he can do any trick at all!

(Use as a finger play. Suggest that children make clown hats. Ask, "Who will be a clown? What funny things can you do? What Western song might the clown sing?")

The Circus Is Coming

The circus is coming, the circus is coming!

Hooray! Hooray!

The circus is coming, the circus is coming,

Today! Today!

Two chimps act so silly. Each one makes a face.

Three fine circus horses are trotting in place.

Four elephants come holding each other's tail,

Walking so slowly along like a snail.

The tigers and grizzly bears growl and they roar.

Two tigers, two bears, and of course that makes four.

The circus is coming, the circus is coming,

Hooray! Hooray!

The circus is coming, the circus is coming

Today! Today!

(The children may have a circus parade as they choose to be two chimpanzees, three horses, four elephants, two tigers, and two bears. Ask them to tell how they would walk and demonstrate the movements. They may make paper bag masks to fit over the head. Recommended reading: I Like Animals by Dahlov Ipcar; Alfred A. Knopf, New York, 1960, Zoo, Where Are You? by Ann McGovern; Harper and Row, New York, 1964, If You Have a Yellow Lion by Susan Purdy; J.B. Lippincott Co., New York, 1966.)

Elephants

One little elephant was playing in the sun.	(Child walks around ring.)
He throught that playing was such a lot of fun,	
He called another elephant and asked him to come.	(A second child joins first.)
Two little elephants were playing in the sun.	
They thought that playing was such a lot of fun,	
They called another elephant and asked her to come.	(A third child joins in.)
Three little elephants were playing in the sun.	
They thought that playing was such a lot of fun,	
They called another elephant and asked him to come.	(A fourth appears.)

140

Continue the game, adding more children until ten are participating. End the rhyme in this way:

Ten little elephants were playing in the sun.

They thought that playing was such a lot of fun,

They didn't call another elephant to come.

-A traditional English rhyme

(Choose ten more children, so each will have a turn.)

This Circus Clown

This circus clown shakes your hand.   (Shake hands.)

This circus clown plays in the band.   (Pretend to play flute.)

This circus clown has enormous feet.   (Show foot.)

This circus clown dearly loves to eat.   (Pretend to eat.)

This circus clown has a round red nose.   (Point to nose.)

This circus clown has white teeth in rows.   (Point to teeth.)

This circus clown has very sad eyes.   (Look sad.)

He laughs, and frowns, and then he cries.   (Demonstrate.)

This circus clown bends away down.   (Bend down.)

What would you do if you were a clown?

(Draw a large clown face on durable tagboard. Color in the features and cut a large opening for the mouth. From a red scrap of felt or colored paper, make a tongue. The children take turns moving the tongue in and out as they make the clown talk. The children will enjoy hearing The Circus Baby *by Maud and Miska Petersham; Macmillan, New York, 1958.)*

Floppety Clown

I am a clown and I don't care a bit

If my pants are pinned and my clothes don't fit.   (Pretend to hold up pants.)

Or if I have a great big toe.   (Show foot.)

(Children) 'Cause I'm a floppety clown, you know.

My arms can flippety, floppety, flap,   (Let arms flap.)

And my head bends down till it touches my lap.   (Bend.)

I twist my body. Look at it go!   (Twist right to left.)

(Children) 'Cause I'm a floppety clown, you know.

Somebody pulls me by a string.   (Stretch neck, pull upward with fingers.)

I open my mouth and start to sing.

My legs are limp and they wobble so.

(Children) 'Cause I'm a floppety clown, you know.

Oh, I can frown and I can smile.

I can stand on my head for a long, long while.

I flip and I flop from head to toe.

(Children) 'Cause I'm a floppety clown, you know.

(Open mouth.)
(Walk unsteadily.)

(Make expressions.)
(Bend head down and touch floor with palms of hands.)
(Flop from side to side.)
(Bow.)

Jo-Jo, The Clown

I can stretch upon my toes,

And hold a ball upon my nose.

(Children) Ha, ha, ha! Ho, ho, ho!

It's fun to be a clown.

(Pantomime actions each time.)

I stand upon my head and shout.

I turn my jacket inside out.

(Children) Ha, ha, ha! Ho, ho, ho!

It's fun to be a clown.

The crowds all clap and shout, "Jo-Jo!

We are so glad you joined the show!"

(Children) Ha, ha, ha! Ho, ho, ho!

It's fun to be a clown.

A funny circus clown am I

And people laugh until they cry!

(Children) Ha, ha, ha! Ho, ho, ho!

It's fun to be a clown.

This Little Clown

This little clown is very fat

This little clown wears a silly hat.

This little clown has a round, red nose.

This little clown has shoes with toes.

This little clown stands upside down.

What is a circus without a clown!

(Children may use clothing from the dress-up box and dramatize the poem, or use as a finger play.)

142

Kangaroo

Old hoppity-loppity kangaroo
Can jump much faster than I or you.

    Hoppity-loppity, jump, one-two.   (Children.)

Her tail is bent like a kitchen chair.
So she can sit down while she combs her hair.

    Hoppity-loppity, jump, one-two.   (Children.)

She has a pouch where her baby grows.
She carries the baby wherever she goes.

    Hoppity-loppity, jump, one-two.   (Children.)

And when she jumps, she uses her tail,
So she can jump farther and almost sail.

    Hoppity-loppity, jump, one-two.   (Children.)

(Give two long jumps, one short one on the word "jump", and two quick jumps on the count: one-two. Place these books on the browsing table: George and Martha by James Marshall, Houghton-Mifflin, Boston, 1972; The Secret Hiding Place by Rainy Bennett, World Publishing Company, Cleveland, 1960.)

Hippopotamus

This hippopotamus looks like a hog.
This hippopotamus is a very large size.
This hippopotamus weights 8000 pounds.
This hippopotamus has very small eyes.

(Read How, Hippo? by Marcia Brown, Charles Scribner's Sons, New York, 1969.)

Here We Go Off to the Zoo

(Tune: *Looby-Loo*)

Here we go off to the zoo,
Here we go off to the zoo,
Here we go off to the zoo, the zoo,
On this beautiful day!
Look at the elephant's nose,
Look at the elephant's nose,

She has a long nose and it works like a hose,
On this beautiful day!
Look at the big baboon,
Look at the big baboon,
He makes faces at you from his cage at the zoo,
On this beautiful day!

Giraffe

Teacher:	Of all of the animals in the zoo,	
	I am the tallest. That is true.	(Reach high.)
Children:	Who am I? I am a giraffe.	
Teacher:	I am brown and white with a little red,	
	And I have two knobs on the top of my head.	(Point fingers at side of head.)
Children:	Who am I? I am a giraffe.	
Teacher:	My neck is long, I am very tall,	
	But I don't have very much voice at all.	(Point to neck.)
Children:	Who am I? I am a giraffe.	
Teacher:	I have one big ear on each side of my head.	
	High up in the air is where I am fed.	
Children:	Who am I? I am a giraffe.	
Teacher:	I walk right up to the tallest tree.	
	And I eat the leaves that are good for me.	
Children:	Who am I? I am a giraffe.	

(Show a picture of a giraffe. Ask, "Have you ever seen a real giraffe? Where? Describe a giraffe. If you could talk to a giraffe, what would you say? What would it say? Can a giraffe drink or pick up something off the ground easily? Why? How can it do so?" - Spread its front legs and bend neck over.)

Five Little Bears

Five little bears were sitting on the ground.	(Five children sit in a row.)
Five little bears made a deep growling sound: Grrrrrr!	(Children growl.)
The first one said, "Let's have a look around."	(One child at a time rises.)
The second one said, "I feel rather funny!"	
The third one said, "I think I smell honey."	
The fourth one said "Shall we climb up the tree?"	
The fifth one said, "Look out! There's a bee!"	
So the five little bears went back to their play,	(Children return to seats.)
And decided to wait till the bees flew away.	

(Dramatize the rhyme with five children taking turns. Give each participant a length of paper on which appear the words to be said. The entire class may say, "The first one said," "The second one said," and so on.)

FROM OTHER LANDS (Foreign Languages)

Most of the main languages in the world are spoken in the United States. In one school alone, there may be several different languages and dialects. Yet there is consolation in knowing that young children can learn a second language quite easily, can absorb expressions that meet their needs, can use practical words repeatedly in real situations, and usually are willing to assume the customs and characteristics of their peer group.

In fact, children can move from one language to another more readily than can an adult. Children are natural imitators of tempo, pitch, and rhythm. They already have learned one language at home by ear. They bring to school no prejudices or inhibitions concerning change.

Most of the new language is learned in social situations. Children devote a large portion of the day in unbroken practice while playing with other children and hearing only English spoken.

This section contains translations. The teacher is advised to use both English and foreign language versions. All rhymes in this book emphasize sounds and sentence patterns we wish all children to practice. The subject will appeal and the unison responses will make learning a second language fun.

Conejo/Rabbit

Conejo, conejo, salta, salta.

Conejo, conejo, detente, detente.

Disculpame hoy,

No puede jugar.

Estoy buscando las hojas de las zanahorias.

-O.M.A.

Rabbit, rabbit, hop, hop, hop.

Rabbit, rabbit, stop, stop, stop.

Excuse me today.

I cannot play.

I am off to look for a carrot top.

Uno, Dos/One, Two

Uno, dos,

Amarrate los zapatos.

Tres, cuatro,

Cierra la puerta.

Cinco, seis,

Da unas pataditos.

Siete, ocho,

Abre la reja.

Nueve, diez,

Cuenta otra vez.

-O.M.A.

One, two,	Give some kicks.
Tie your shoe.	Seven, eight,
Three, four,	Open the gate.
Shut the door.	Nine, ten,
Five, six,	Count again.

145

¿Que Tu Ves?/What Do You See?

Mira, mira, ¿que tu ves?

Veo un nido de pájaro en lo alto del árbol.

Mira, mira, ¿que tu ves?

Veo una flor y un abejarrón.

Mira, mira, ¿que tu ves?

Veo un amiguito saludandome.

-O.M.A.

Look, look what do you see?

I see a bird's nest up in a tree.

Look, look, what do you see?

I see a flower and a bumblebee.

Look, look, what do you see?

I see a little friend waving at me.

Contando/Counting

Uno, uno, contar es divertido.

Dos, dos, lo contaré para tí.

Tres, tres, cuenta por mí.

Cuatro, cuatro, vamos a contar un poco mas.

-O.M.A.

One, one, counting is fun.

Two, two, I'll count for you.

Three, three, you count for me.

Four, four, let's count some more.

Toca Cinco Campanas/Ring Five Bells

¡Toca las campanas, toca las campanas,

Este es el día de Navidad!   (Repita.)

Uno es para el pesebre

Dos es para la paja.

Tres es para la estrella brillante

Que señala el camino.   (Repita el coro.)

Cuatro es para los pastores,

Quienes vieron la luz de los angeles.

Cinco es para el Nino pequeño

Quien nació ese feliz noche.

¡Toca las campanas, toca las campanas,

Este es el diá de Navidad!

Ring the bells, ring the bells,

This is Christmas Day!   (Repeat.)

One is for the manger,

Two is for the hay,

Three is for the shining star
That pointed out the way.
Four is for the shepherds
Who saw the angel light.
Five is for the little Boy
Born that happy night.
Ring the bells, ring the bells,
This is Christmas Day!

(Repeat the chorus.)

-O.M.A.

Dos Patitos/Two Ducks

Dos patitos se encontraron.   (Move two fingers toward each other.)

El patito graznó: ¿Por donde vas, amigo?   (Wiggle right thumb.)

El patito graznó: Voy a la escuela.   (Wiggle left thumb.)

¿Por donde vas, amigo?   (Wiggle left thumb.)

Voy a mi casa.   (Wiggle right thumb.)

Adiós.   (Place right thumb behind back.)

Adiós.   (Place left thumb behind back.)

Two ducks met.   (Move two fingers toward each other.)

Little duck quacked, "Where are you going, my   (Wiggle right thumb.)
friend?"

Little duck quacked, "I am going to school."   (Wiggle left thumb.)

"Where are you going, my friend?"   (Wiggle left thumb.)

"I am going home."   (Wiggle right thumb.)

"Good-by."   (Place right thumb behind back.)

"Good-by."   (Place left thumb behind back.)

Two Rhymes from Turkey

Bir eekie, dir bir eekee
On eekie dir, on eekee.
In anmas san soli da bac.

It is one. It is one.   (Hold up one finger.)

It is twelve, it is twelve.   (Point to numeral on the board.)

If you do not agree,

Count and see!

147

Meg yergoo, yergunnas;

Yerec chors chornas;

Hinc, vetz, vernas;

Yoten ooten, ooranas;

Innin dacenin, jam yertas;

Dac yergoo, hatz geran.

One, two, stand up tall,

Three, four, sink down.

Five, six, sit up.

Seven, eight, say nothing at all.

Nine, ten, go to church.

Eleven, twelve, go to supper.

¿Qué Colores Veo?/What Colors Do I See?

¡Veo, veo, veo!

¿Qué colores veo?

Ciruelas moradas,	(Point to thumb.)
Tomates rojos,	(Point to second finger.)
Maiz amarillo,	(Point to middle finger.)
Patatas cafes,	(Point to fourth finger.)
Lechuga verde,	(Point to fifth finger.)

¡Ay qué delicioses!

Todos los colores

Que aprendo al comer.

See, see, see!

What colors do I see?

Purple plums,	(Point to thumb.)
Red tomatoes,	(Point to second finger.)
Yellow corn,	(Point to middle finger.)
Brown potatoes,	(Point to fourth finger.)
Green lettuce!	(Point to fifth finger.)

Yum, yum, yum, good!

I learn so many colors

When I eat my food!

Con las Manos/With the Hands

Con las manos
Aplaudo, aplaudo, aplaudo   (Clap hands three times.)
Y ahora las pongo
En mi regazo.   (Fold hands in lap.)

With my hands
I clap, clap, clap   (Clap hands three times.)
And now I lay them
In my lap.   (Fold hands in lap.)

J'Irai Dans le Bois/To the Woods Goes She

Un, deux, trois, j'irai dans le bois,
Quatre, cinq, six, chercher les cerises,
Sept, huit, neuf, dans mon panier neuf,
Dix, onze, douze, elles seront toutes rouges.

One, two, three, to the woods goes she;
Four, five, six, cherries she picks;
Seven, eight, nine, in her basket fine;
Ten, eleven, twelve, she said,
All the cherries are red, red, red!

-Traditional

La Mariposa/The Butterfly

Uno, dos, tres, cuatro, cinco,   (Pop up fingers on the right hand as you count.)
Cogí una mariposa de un brinco.
Seis, siete, ocho, neuve, diez,   (Pop up fingers on the left hand as you count.)
La solte brincando otra vez.

-O.M.A.

One, two, three, four, five,   (Pop up fingers on the right hand as you count.)
I caught a butterfly.
Six, seven, eight, nine, ten,   (Pop up fingers on the left hand as you count.)
I let him go again.

Italian Lullaby

Bimbo, bimbo, piccolino;   Uno, due, tre,
Bello, bello, ditolino.   quattro, cinque.
Quanti, quanti, ce ne sono?   Batti, batti le manin,   -Traditional
Uno, due, tre,   Forte, forte, angelin!
quattro, cinque, qui—

(Continued next page)

Baby, baby, little as can be;
Hold your fingers up for me.
How many fingers do we see?
One, two, three, four, five on the left.
One, two, three, four, five on the right.
Clap them now
With all your might!

Eins, Zwei/One, Two

Eins, zwei, Polizei;	(Touch two thumbs together.)
Drei, vier, Offizier;	(Touch two pointer fingers together.)
Funf, sechs, alte Hex:	(Touch two middle fingers together.)
Sieben, acht, gute nacht;	(Touch two ring fingers together.)
Neun, zehn, auf wiedersehen.	(Touch two little fingers together.)
One, two, policemen blue;	(Touch two thumbs together.)
Three, four, captain of the corps;	(Touch two pointer fingers together.)
Five, six, a witch on sticks;	(Touch two middle fingers together.)
Seven, eight, the hour is late;	(Touch two ring fingers together.)
Nine, ten, till we meet again.	(Touch two little fingers together.)

-Traditional

Ardilla/Squirrel

Ardilla, ardilla, sentada en el árbol,
Ardilla, ardilla, baja y ven a mí.
Mi armiguita, como tu ves
Yo tengo tres ardillitas y por lo tanto
No puede jugar aqui.

-O.M.A.

Squirrel, squirrel, up in a tree,
Squirrel, squirrel come down to me.
My little friend, I thought you knew
I have three baby squirrels so
I cannot play with you.

A Japanese Game

Hana, hana, hana, kuchi;
Kuchi, kuchi, kuchi, mimi;
Mimi, mimi, mimi, me.

Nose, nose, nose, mouth;
Mouth, mouth, mouth, ear;
Ear, ear, ear, eye.

-Traditional

Months of the Year

Uno es enero para el invierno.
Dos es febrero para la nieve.
Tres es marzo para el viento.
Cuatro es abril para la lluvia.
Cinco es mayo para las flores.
Seis es junio para el parque.
Siete es julio para la playa.
Ocho es agosto para el zoológico.
Nueve es septiembre para la escuela.
Diez es octubre para la espiritu errante.
Once es noviembre para el pavo.
Doce es diciembre para la Navidad y Hanukkah.

-O.M.A.

One is January for winter.
Two is February for snow.
Three is March for wind.
Four is April for rain.
Five is May for flowers.

Six is June for the park.

Seven is July for the beach.

Eight is August for the zoo.

Nine is September for school.

Ten is October for the goblin.

Eleven is November for the turkey.

Twelve is December for Christmas and Hanukkah.

COMMUNITY FRIENDS AND HELPERS

To enable a child to make necessary challenges concerning changes in our community, the school will create favorable attitudes toward the people who work for
us in our own neighborhoods and cities. These individuals work constructively to
help make a good functioning place for us to live and work.

From the home, a child has learned ways of behavior and ways of feeling. The
teacher now branches out to the community and asks, "What is a neighbor? Who
helps make our neighborhood? Who serves us? What would happen if we had no
postal workers? no electricians? no telephone workers? no gas meter readers? no
teachers?" Children then learn about the cobbler and the baker in rhyme and
they begin to understand and appreciate the contributions these people make.

Different People

This person drives a taxi.

This person leads a band.

This person guides the traffic

By holding up a hand.

This person brings the letters.

This person rakes and hoes.

This person is a funny clown

Who dances on tiptoes.

*(Invite the children to choose which person he/
she would like to be and pantomime the action,
asking the class to identify the worker. Ask the
child to use no words, only hands, feet, and bodies. Ask, "Did we leave out anyone? Who? Shall
we add your person to the poem? What rhymes
with hand? - band; with hoes? - tiptoes.")*

The Window Cleaner

Up goes the ladder to the side of the wall.

Don't worry! The window cleaner won't fall.

A window cleaner goes up to the top

(Fingers simulate climbing by turning wrists
and touching thumbs.)

(Continued next page)

151

Up and on the last rung he'll/she'll stop.

He/she polishes the windows and makes them shine.

And when he/she is done, he/she will say, "That is fine!"

(Ask "Have you ever watched a window cleaner at work? Tell about it." Explain the word rung *on a ladder and* have rung *a bell.)*

Hats They Wear

This person wears a helmet when he/she plays football.

This person wears a Western hat that is quite wide and tall.

This person wears a top hat like Abraham Lincoln wore.

This person wears a hunter's hat when he/she goes to explore.

This person wears a baseball cap so snugly on his/her head.

This person is a firefighter with helmet that is red.

This person, like George Washington, wears a three-cornered hat.

This person is a sailor whose hat is short and flat.

This person wears a bonnet for he/she is six months old.

This person wears a fur hat in weather that is cold.

(The children hold up one finger at a time until ten are shown. Ask, "What kind of hat do you like best? Would you like to make a hat for yourself? What kind?" Show pictures of the various hats. Encourage participation.)

Telephone Line Workers

Over the towns and countryside

Telephone wires stretch far and wide.   (Hands measure width.)

This first line worker climbs a pole   (Motion of climbing with hands.)

With bravery and self-control.

The second wears goggles on his/her eyes   (Fingers encircle eyes.)

In case some steel from wire flies.

The third one wears a belt with pride.   (Circle waist with two hands.)

A safety belt is his/her best guide.

The fourth one climbs in cold and heat

With safe, strong climbers on both feet.   (Show feet one at a time.)

The fifth, a telephone installs

Just so that you can make your calls.   (Hand to ear.)

(This rhyme may be used as a finger play to review ordinal numbers. Discuss community helpers with the class. Encourage oral participation.)

Signs

This sign says, "Keep off the grass."

This sign says, "Do not pass."

This sign says, "Stop! Light is red!"

This sign says, "One lane ahead."

This sign says, "Yellow—slow!"

This sign says, "Green light, go."

This sign says, "This paint is new."

This sign says, "This way to the zoo."

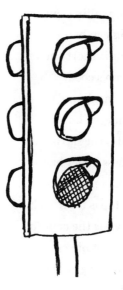

(Actual signs to be made can be held up and the rhyme dramatized. Encourage a discussion of signs and ask the children to think of others such as "Beware of the Dog." Although the words may be difficult for the child to master, the class can say "This sign says" in unison. Children may also hold up one finger at a time to simulate signs. Have a discussion on why signs are necessary. "Do we have any signs here at school?" - Exit, Boy's and Girl's Rest Room, Wet Paint, Keep Off.)

Workers

This worker feeds the lions at the zoo.

This worker drives an engine to the fire.

This worker makes a new sole for your shoe.

This worker mends a high electric wire.

This worker drives a sweeper through the streets.

This worker bakes a cookie or a bun.

This worker sells my parents food to eat,

And I'm very glad we've got them, every one!

("Think of other people in the community who help us. What is a person who sells meat called? the person who fixes an electric wire? the person who mends shoes? the person who sells cookies and buns? Shall we say the rhyme together? Let your fingers tell how many people help us." Encourage oral participation.)

Ten Clerks

One clerk works hard unpacking beans and rice.

Two clerks work hard arranging all the spice.

Three clerks work hard wrapping yellow cheese.

Four clerks work hard sorting drinks and teas.

Five clerks work hard marking all the jam.

Six clerks work hard slicing up the ham.

Seven clerks work hard packaging the sweets.

Eight clerks work hard selling all the meats.

Nine clerks work hard shelving rolls and bread.

Ten clerks worn out go home to bed.

(Show the correct number of fingers at a time. Ask: "What else does a supermarket clerk do?" Visit a supermarket and ask the manager what the workers do. Encourage pupil participation in saying the rhyme.)

Five Little Sailors

Five little sailors are going out to sea
In their little sailing ship
As sturdy as can be.

The first one is short and fat;   (Point to thumb.)
He is the ship's cook.
He gets the meals and uses
As excellent cook book.

The second is the navigator.   (Indicate pointer finger.)
With compass in her hand.
The compass tells directions,
When the ship is far from land.

The third one is the captain.   (Point to middle finger.)
Who has a great big crew.
He sees that things run smoothly.
And he tells them what to do.

The fourth one is the first mate,   (Point to ring finger.)
The fifth, the cabin boy.   (Point to small finger.)
They sail off over the ocean blue
Shouting, "SHIP AHOY!"   (Everyone shouts "Ship Ahoy!")

(Read the rhyme to the class before asking them to participate. Ask "How many members of the crew can you remember?" With hands on hips, children take two steps to the right, two to the left, and salute. Suggest that volunteers choose parts and dramatize the rhyme.)

The Cobblers

With a rap-a-tap-tap,
And a rap-a-tap-too!
The cobblers are mending
My worn-out shoe.

The first fixes soles.
He's the hammer man.
The second mends heels,
As only she can.

The third makes an eye
Where the string goes through.
The fourth dyes the leather
Brown, red, or blue.
The fifth cobbler sews

With a tiny, tiny needle.
With a rap-a-tap-tap,
And a tick-a-tack-teedle!
With a rap-a-tap-tap,
And a rap-a-tap-too!
Without the shoe cobblers,
What would we do?

(Bring in a shoe to demonstrate its parts. The shoe in the rhyme has shoestrings, so sneakers will do. After reading the rhyme, ask "What does the first cobbler do? the second? the third? Have you ever visited a cobbler's shop to have your shoes mended? What was wrong with your shoes? How does the cobbler help us save money in our community?")

154

The Mail

The postal delivery person comes around each day.

She/he leaves all of our letters and then goes on her/his way.

So six mysterious letters were lying on a tray.

Daddy came and looked at them and then took one away.

Mother said, "This business letter surely is for me."

My sister took a letter, and now there are just _____.

Puppy looked all around to see if there was mail.

She jumped up and she took one, then she wagged her little tail.

My brother Arnie took one, it was next one to the last.

He ran upstairs two at a time and opened it real fast.

Baby said, "There is one left and I am only three,

Of course I cannot read yet, but maybe it's for me."

(Substitute names of children in the class. Use cancelled envelopes for letters and dramatize the rhyme. As you read the rhyme a second time, ask the class to tell how many letters are left each time. Make up a rhyme about what Baby did with her letter. Write on the board: "Six minus _____ equals _____." Children enjoy playing a delivery person.)

Jackets

This jacket has five buttons

That button me inside.

This jacket has a zipper

With pocket on each side.

This jacket has a letter

That shows I'm on a team.

This jacket is for drivers

That come to sell ice cream.

(Cut the tops from large grocery bags. Cut armholes in the sacks so that children can wear them and decorate them from the odds and ends box. Alternate use for a finger play. Make a scrapbook containing zippers children can zip, sewed-in pockets they can fill with objects, and a heavy cloth strip with holes through which buttons can be slipped. Sew buttons on another cloth strip so that children can practice this exercise for finger dexterity.)

Making Clothes

Six little mice at their spinning wheels,   (Whirl hands.)

Working away with happy squeals.   (Children say "Squeak" three times.)

Two ran into a hole in the floor.

How many are left? Why, there are _____.   (Children supply number.)

Four little mice at their spinning wheels,   (Repeat motions.)

Working away with happy squeals.   (Squeak.)

Two of the mice saw a furry cap

They climbed inside and took a nap.   (Children tell how many remain.)

Two little mice at their spinning wheels,   (Repeat action.)

Working away with happy squeals.

The rest of the mice then ran away.

They will all come back another day.

Yes, because spinning is their trade.

They all like clothes that are ready made!

(Say, "Pretend to be mice at your spinning wheels. Make happy squeals. What are 'ready-made' clothes? Who makes your clothes? Do you buy all of them at a store?")

(Squeak.)

(Children tell how many remain.)

Five Hats

Child 1: The first hat is mine.

I wear it for fun.

I bought it myself

It keeps off the sun.

Child 2: This second hat's fine.

It suits me just so.

And I take it with me

Wherever I go.

Child 3: This third hat I like

Because of its crown;

And it has a brim

I can turn up and down.

Child 4: The fourth hat is nice.

It is not like the rest;

But I wear it the most

'Cause I like it the best.

Child 5: The fifth hat, of course,

It covers my head.

I don't take it off

Until I go to bed.

(Children may bring hats to school to dramatize this poem. Suggest that parents donate hats you can lay on a table. Individuals choose which hats they want to wear. The child who volunteers for a stanza says as much as he/she can remember. Use as a finger play if desired.)

Five Sugar Buns

Five sugar buns in the baker's shop,

Big and round with icing on top.

Along came _____ with a dime one day,

She/he bought a sugar bun and took it away.

Four sugar buns in the baker's shop,

Big and round with icing on top.

Along came _____ with a dime one day.

She/he bought a sugar bun and took it away.

Continue the sequence, three sugar buns, and so on. End the rhyme in this way:

No sugar buns in the baker's shop,

Big and round with icing on top.

Please, Mister Baker, bake once again,

And this time bake eight, nine or ten.

-Traditional

(Make sure that five children at a time have turns.)

The Dentist

When I try to count my teeth,	(Point to teeth.)
I count and count and then,	
I have to rest; I've done my best,	
I counted up to ten.	
One, two, three, four, five, six, seven,	(Children point to teeth and count.)
Eight, nine, ten.	
I then go to the dentist	
And let her see my teeth.	(Open mouth.)
She pumps the chair up to my size	
With a pedal underneath.	
Up and down the pedal goes,	(Raise hand up and down several times.)
And so I take a ride.	
And then I open up my mouth	(Open mouth.)
So she can see inside.	
She says to me, "Well, one, two, three,	(Count on fingers.)
Four, five, six, seven, and eight.	
It all looks fine except	
For two that must look straight."	(Hold up two fingers.)

(Ask: "What will happen to the two teeth that are not straight, but crooked? Have you ever known anyone to wear braces to straighten teeth? What do you do to help keep your teeth clean? If we never went to a dentist, what might happen?")

Four Busy Firefighters

Four busy firefighters could not retire	(Hold up four fingers.)
Because they might have to put out a fire.	
The first one rang a big brass bell.	(Point to one finger at a time.)
The second one said, "It's the Grand Hotel!"	
The third one said, "Down the pole we'll slide."	
The fourth one said, "Get ready to ride."	
The siren said, "Get out of the way!	
We have to put out a fire today!"	
The red fire truck speeded on to the fire,	
As the big yellow flames grew higher and higher.	
Swish went the water from the fire-hose spout,	
And in no time at all, the fire was out.	

The people all clapped and they gave a big yell:

"The firefighters saved our Grand Hotel!"

(Dramatize the rhyme. Children who can read may play the firefighters and fire engine and read the words you may write on strips of paper or on the board. The rest of the class may be people. For those children who cannot read, memorization will be easy when the rhyme is repeated. Children enjoy playing "fire engine.")

Painting

Paint the ceiling, paint the door,

Paint the walls, and paint the floor.

Paint the roof - slush, slush, slush!

Paint the doorstep with your brush.

Now my house is done, you see.

You may come and visit me.

I've been working very hard

To paint my playhouse

In the yard.   (Sit on floor.)

(Pantomime the action of painting. Ask, "What else would you paint if you were painting a house?" Ask for rhyming words.)

Windows

This house has many windows,

And some are very wide.   (Measure with hands.)

This one looks cross and frowning.   (Make frowning expression.)

You dare not look inside.

This window looks quite happy.   (More expressions.)

This window looks quite sad.

This window is so beautiful

It makes us all feel glad.

This window has bright curtains.

This window looks so bare.

This window looks inviting.

I wonder who lives there!

(This rhyme can also be used as a finger play. Suggest that children draw pictures of the windows with various expressions.)

I Want to be a Carpenter

I want to be a carpenter and work the whole day long.

I'll use a great big box of tools; my arms are very strong.

First, I'll saw and saw and saw, and cut the boards in two.

Little boards and big boards—all kinds of boards will do.

I'll plane and plane and plane the boards for every one is rough.

Back and forth I'll plane the boards until they're smooth enough.

I'll measure them and measure them—each one down to a T,

And then I'll start to build a house for me up in a tree!

(Children pantomime the actions. Ask, "Have you seen a treehouse? Have you been in one? Describe it. Would you like to have one? Why? What kinds of tools would anyone need to build a treehouse? How do you get up to a treehouse?" Encourage verbal participation.)

Our Community Helpers

Some people bring us produce,

And drinks all fresh and cold.

Some people work in shops and stores

Where many things are sold.

Some people bring us letters and

They take more mail away.

Some people stop the traffic

To help us on own way.

Some people move our furniture,

And put it in a van.

Some people take the garbage,

And empty every can.

(Ask pupils to tell what other people do to help us. "What does a weather person do? A sailor that goes to sea?" Let them choose the helpers they would like to be when they grow up. Bring in pictures of different community workers for the bulletin board.)

THE FARM

Five Little Mice

L.B.S.

1. Five lit-tle mice ran out to the farm, Out to the farm one day. One lit-tle mouse heard a bow-wow-wow! And she scam-pered a-way, a-way.

1. Five little mice ran out to the farm,
   Out to the farm one day.
   One little mouse heard a bow-wow-wow!
   And she scampered away, away!

2. Four little mice ran out to the farm,
   Out to the farm one day.
   One little mouse heard a mew-mew-mew!
   And she scampered away, away!

3. Three little mice ran out to the farm,
   Out to the farm one day.
   One little mouse heard a quack, quack, quack!
   And he scampered away, away!

4. Two little mice ran out to the farm,
   Out to the farm one day.
   One little mouse heard a baa-baa-baa!
   And he scampered away, away!

5. One little mouse ran out to the farm,
   Out to the farm one day.
   That little mouse heard a cock-a-doodle-doo!
   And scampered away, away.

6. No little mice are out on the farm,
   Out on the farm today.
   Let's bring them all back. 1,2,3,4,5.
   And we hope that the mice will stay.

(One child at a time runs away; all children return for sixth verse.)

Ducks

Ten fat ducks came waddling down the lane.

     Quack, quack, quack! Quack, quack, quack!   (Children say this refrain after each line.)

Two marched off to paddle in the rain.

Eight fat ducks came waddling down the path.

Two marched off to take a shower bath.

Six fat ducks came waddling down the road.

Two chased after a big brown toad.

Four fat ducks came waddling down the street.

Two ran off to find some bugs to eat.

Two fat ducks came waddling down the hill.

With a big duck smile on each duck bill.

The last two ducks waddled back to the hill.

With a big duck smile on each duck bill.

The next two ducks came back to the road.

They gave up chasing the big brown toad.

The next two ducks came back to the street.

Glad that they'd found some bugs to eat.

The next two ducks came back to the path.

With feathers still wet from their fine shower
bath.

The next two ducks came back to the lane.

And all ten ducks were together once again.

(The children repeat the refrain: "Quack, quack, quack! Quack, quack, quack!" Choose ten children to play the ducks and walk around the room as they play the action. They leave two at a time and return in the same way. At the end of the rhyme, all come together on the rug so that ten other children have a turn. Since all ducks would be the same, use a duck pattern. Ask the children to cut ten ducks, and say the poem with you as they place the figures on the flannelboard. This selection teaches children to add by two's and take away by two's.)

My Puppy

Here is a roof

On top of a house.

Who lives here?

Is it a mouse?

Here is a collar.

Is it for a cat?

No, it's all for my puppy

So cuddly and fat.

(Point index fingers together.)

(Place one hand on top of the other.)

(Hands encircle neck.)

The Hard-Working Farmer

What does the farmer give us to eat?

He/she gives us our bread that is made from wheat.

He/she gives us our beans and our ripe tomatoes.

He/she gives us our cabbage and our potatoes.

He/she gives us the cows for the milk each day.

He/she raises the soybeans and oats and hay.

He/she raises the corn we can eat from the cob.

He/she sees that everyone has a job.

He/she works all day till the set of sun,

And his/her family helps him/her, every one!

(Ask the children to tell what else a farmer does. If children are in a farm area, they will be able to add many ideas to this rhyme. Ask for words that rhyme with eat, *with* hay, *with* sun, *with* tomatoes. *Ask individuals to recall as many events as possible from the rhyme. Listen for the plurals at the ends of words like* tomatoes, *and so on.)*

The Farmer Works

The farmer works hard every day.

He/she rakes the leaves. He/she rakes the hay.

He/she gets up when the rooster crows,

And with a tractor plows long rows.

He/she shears the sheep and feeds the hens.

He/she milks the cows and cleans the pens.

He/she cuts the wood to use for fuel.

He/she takes care of his/her favorite mule.

He/she raises corn and oats and wheat.

He/she grows the food we like to eat.

(Ask the children to explain how the farmer would rake the yard. What would he/she do with the hay? Which pens would need cleaning? How does a tractor help the farmer? The farmer drives a tractor, and plants and tends the gardens. He/she takes care of the animals. Ask, "If you were part of a farmer's family, how would you help? While I read the rhyme again, count how many things the farmer does.")

One Old Man Went to Mow

One old man went to mow,

Went to mow in the meadow.

One man and his dog Spot,

Went to mow in the meadow.

Two old men went to mow,

Went to mow in the meadow.

Two men, one man, and his dog Spot

Went to mow in the meadow.

Three old men went to mow,

Went to mow in the meadow.

Three men, two men, one man, and his dog Spot

Went to mow in the meadow.

-Adapted from an old English rhyme

(Use as many children in the class as desired. Continue until ten "men" are chosen. One child may be the dog Spot and follow behind the others as they march around the room.)

162

Cows on a Farm

This cow has a nose that is soft as silk.

This cow gives a pail of good sweet milk.

This cow switches flies with her long, thin tail.

This cow eats corn and hay by the bale.

This cow at night, sleeps inside a stall.

This cow has a baby calf very small.

The farmer says, "I don't know how

I could run this farm without a fine cow!"

(Children point to one finger at a time. Ask, "Have you visited a farm? Have you seen a cow? What does a farmer's family do to help on the farm? Why does the farmer say that a cow is so important?")

Six Young Roosters

Six young roosters began to play;

When all of a sudden, one ran away.

Five young roosters began to crow;

When all of a sudden, one hurt his toe.

Four young roosters went to the fair,

When all of a sudden, one wasn't there.

Three young roosters, and just as I feared,

All of a sudden, one disappeared!

Two young roosters pecked on the ground;

When all of a sudden, one couldn't be found.

One young rooster went to his nest;

When all of a sudden, he found all the rest.

(Ask for volunteers to play the six roosters. They sit on a rug representing a set. One at a time leaves and at the end all return. All say the line "When all of a sudden," until they are more familiar with the rhyme. Read Rickety Rackety Rooster *by Jean Wall; Simon and Schuster, New York, 1968.)*

The Old Woman and Her Friends

There was an old woman who lived on a hill,

On top of a hill where winds gave her a chill.

She had for a neighbor one little field mouse

In a hole underneath the floor of her house.

Two rabbits lived near her. Their fur was dark gray.

She fed them some carrots almost every day.

Then there were three puppies. She was not alone.

And she gave every puppy a nice, juicy bone.

Four pigs came along and they lived in her barn.

The pigs got quite fat for they ate too much corn.

Sometimes the old woman would tire and doze.

And five flies would rest on the end of her nose.

Now the birds have all gone and the cold winter blows,

She makes six snow people and gives them some clothes.

(With the number of characters involved, you may wish to use this rhyme as a dramatization and mathematical lesson on sets. One child plays the old woman. One mouse, two rabbits, three puppies, four pigs, and five flies make set groupings in various sections of the room. They visit the old woman who feeds them pantomimically. Each set may carry its own sign of identification. Ask the class: "How many are in each set? What do you like about the old woman? Would you like being her friend? Why? Do you think the old woman was lonely? Why?" Read What Do the Animals Say? *by Grace Shaar; Scholastic, New York, 1972.)*

Animals on the Farm

One little mouse, squeakety-squeak.

Two little kittens peekety-peek.

Three little puppies, boo-woo-woo!

Four little roosters, cock-a-doodle-doo!

Five old hens, clack, clack, clack.

Six fat ducks, quack, quack, quack!

(Children are chosen to play the roles of one mouse, two kittens, etc. Each group may make the animal sounds. Ask, "How would a mouse move? a duck? a rooster?")

Five Little Pigs

L.B.S.

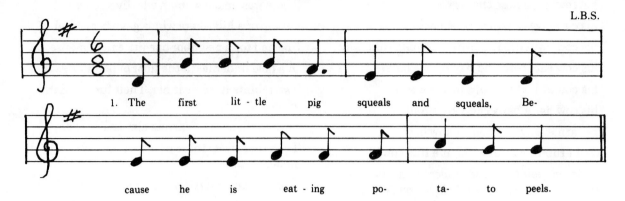

1. The first lit - tle pig squeals and squeals, Be-

cause he is eat - ing po - ta - to peels.

1. The first little pig squeals and squeals,
   Because he is eating potato peels.

2. The next little pig with a curly tail
   Is drinking her milk from a shiny pail.

3. The third little pig just likes to play.
   She rolls and rolls in the mud all day.

4. The fourth little pig is just a runt.
   But he is the one with the loudest grunt.

5. The fifth little pig says, "I will share
   My lunch with you for I've some to spare."

6. Five little pigs are in their pen,
   So now shall we count them all over again?

All say: 1, 2, 3, 4, 5
          Why, they are the cutest pigs alive!

(Children volunteer to line up and pretend to be pigs. Everyone sings. Recommended reading: A Treeful of Pigs *by Arnold Lobel; Greenwillow, New York, 1979.)*

This Is the Farm

This is the meadow where every day	(Spread hands.)
Many farm animals come to play.	
Here is the food that the farmer brings.	(Cup hands.)
Hay, oats, and corn and other good things.	
Here is a great, big watering trough.	(Measure with hands.)
They take a long drink and then scamper off.	(Fingers move.)
Here are the shears that shear the sheep.	(Movement of cutting.)
So that we might have blankets for sleep.	
Here is the barn where they all unite	(Point fingers together.)
To rest themselves and sleep all night.	

(Practice the sentences using "Here are" and "Here is.")

164

On the Farm

Here is a piggie fat and round.

He uses his snout to dig up the ground.

Here is a rooster-pooster, too.

He crows with a "Cock-a-doodle-doo!"

Here is a cow who gives us milk.

Her nose is cold and as soft as silk.

Here is a sheep. "Baa-baa" she goes.

She gives us the wool to make our clothes.

Here is a quacking baby duck.

Here is a hen that says, "Cluck, cluck!"

(Hold up one finger at a time. Ask, "Which one would you like for a pet? Of what use are these animals on a farm? Of what use are they to us?" - Cow gives milk, chicken lays eggs.)

Four Billy Goats

The first billy goat climbs on the roof.

The second billy goat taps with his hoof.

The third billy goat doesn't want to wait.

The fourth billy goat opens up the gate.

Four billy goats get into the garden

And don't even say, "I beg your pardon."

(Point to one finger at a time. Write "They don't" and "He doesn't" on the board and use for drill of verb forms. Sing "Three Little Ducklings" from More Singing Fun *by Lucille F. Wood and Louise Binder Scott; Bowmar/Noble, Los Angeles, 1954.)*

Five Yellow Ducklings

Five yellow ducklings	
Dash, dash, dash!	(Clap three times.)
Jumped in the duck pond,	(Make jumping motion.)
Splash, splash, splash!	(Clap three times.)
Heads went down,	(Move hand down.)
And tails went swish!	(Move palms upward quickly.)
They all said "Hello"	
To a big, black fish.	(Make swimming motion.)
Mother duck called them,	
"Quack, quack, quack,"	(Clap three times.)
And all five ducklings	
Swam right back.	(Swimming motion again.)

-From *More Singing Fun* by Lucille F. Wood and
Louise Binder Scott; Bowmar/Noble, Los Angeles, 1954.

Five Young Ducklings

Five young ducks went out to play

Over the hills and far away.

Mother Duck called them,

"Quack, quack, quack."

But only four little ducks came back.

Four little ducks went out to play

Over the hills and far away.

Mother Duck called them,

"Quack, quack, quack."

But only three little ducks came back.

Continue the rhyme until no ducks return. End the rhyme in this way:

Old Mother Duck went out one day

Over the hills and far away.

She called all her babies,

"Quack, quack, quack."

And all of the five little ducks came back.

(Recommended reading: Make Way for Ducklings *by Robert McCloskey; Puffin Books, New York, 1941.)*

Little Goslings

One little gosling hatched today.

Two little goslings walked this way: (Children do a waddling walk.)

Three little goslings said, "Peep, peep!" (Children imitate.)

Four little goslings went to sleep. (Hands beside head.)

Five little goslings ate some grain. (Motion of eating.)

Six little goslings liked the cool rain. (Hands raised and lowered.)

Seven little goslings swam in the lake. (Motion of swimming.)

Eight little goslings gave their wings a shake. (Move arms up and down.)

Nine little goslings ran around and played.

They will be big, fat geese some day.

(Point to one finger at a time. The word gosling *can be changed to* duckling *and* quacking *used instead of* peeping. *If there is a pattern, a gosling shape can be traced by each child. They can color, cut them out, back them with construction paper and then fine sandpaper, and use them on the flannelboard.)*

Five Hens Learning to Cook

Five old hens were learning how to cook.

They said, "We'll use the recipes in our cook book."

But one old hen went out to the store.

She forgot what to buy, so then there were
_____.

Four old hens were learning how to cook.

They said, "We'll use the recipes in our cook book."

One old hen found a splendid recipe.

She dropped it in the soup, so then there were
_____.

Three old hens were learning how to cook.

They said, "We'll use the recipes in our cook book."

But one old hen was making oyster stew.

She put in sugar by mistake, and then there
were _____.

Two old hens were learning how to cook.

They said, "We'll use the recipes in our cook book."

One old hen made a lovely sugar bun.

She burned it to a crisp, so then there was
_____.

One old hen just put the kettle on,

She had some tea all by herself. The other hens had gone.

Five old hens never learned how to cook.

They wouldn't read directions in their new cook book.

(Bring in a portable electric oven and bake some frozen cookies. Watch them rise and when done, see that each child has a taste. Ask, "Why were the old hens so foolish? Do you have a cook book at home? Do you ever help your mother/father cook? Why is it a good idea to have a cook book?")

(Children supply the number.)

Farmer Jones' Farm

One dog,

Two cats,

Three goats,

And four white rats.

Five hens,

Six cows,

Seven geese,

And eight sows.

Nine sheep,

Ten lambs,

    And hidden away where nobody sees,

    Are a hundred and fifty honey bees!

This Little Chicken

This little chicken was the first to hatch.

This little chicken found a place to scratch.

This little chicken made her two eyes blink.

This little chicken took a long, cool drink.

This little chicken cried, "Peep, peep, peep!"

This little chicken went fast asleep.

The mother called to the tiny things,

And they all crept under her warm, soft wings.

(Point to one finger at a time or use cutouts on the flannelboard. If children say dis *for* this, *encourage practice on the words; do the same for a child who substitutes* w *for* l *in* little.*)*

Five Little Ducks

Five little ducks went for a swim.

The first little duck dived right in.

The second little duck swam around and back.

The third little duck said, "Quack, quack!"

The fourth little duck said to her brother,

"Let's find our mother. There is no other."

(Ask, "What is a father duck called?" - drake. "Show how you would dive right into the water without touching the floor. Show how you would swim. Show us the first finger, the second, third, fourth, and fifth.")

Hatching Chickens

Five eggs and five eggs	(Hold up one hand and then the other.)
Are underneath a hen.	
Five eggs and five eggs,	(Hold up all fingers.)
And that makes ten.	
The hen keeps the eggs warm for three long weeks.	(Hold up three fingers.)
Snap go the shells with tiny little beaks.	(Snap fingers.)
Crack, crack the shells go.	(Clap four times.)
The chickens everyone	
Fluff out their feathers	
In the warm spring sun.	(Make circle of arms.)

Frisky Little Ponies

One little pony so full of fun

Likes to whinny and trot and run.

Two little ponies eat oats from a trough.

And when they are full, they gallop off.

Three little ponies like their snacks

Before they will give us rides on their backs.

(After reading the rhyme, ask the class to say the first part of each line. Ask volunteers how they would trot, gallop, run, and whinny. The rhyme may be dramatized.)

The Adventures of Little Mice

Five little mice looked for something to eat.

They wanted to have a wonderful treat.

The first little mouse nibbled at a slice

Of warm, fresh bread and it tasted nice.

The second little mouse nibbled at a cake.

He ate fast and got a tummy ache,

The third little mouse nibbled at a pie.

It tasted sweet and she gave a sigh.

The fourth little mouse nibbled at a cheese

The fifth little mouse said, "Be quiet, please.

I hear someone coming to open the door!"

So they all hid under a board in the floor.

(Five children dramatize the rhyme. It can be used as a finger play and to review ordinals. Ask, "How would you act if you had a 'tummy' ache? How would you give a big sigh? Who will tell the other mice to be quiet in a soft voice?")

CREATURES TO LOVE

A relationship with animals can be of great value to a child. Kindness to animals that respond to love is an enriching and a rewarding experience.

In a New York City zoo, where children were allowed to take home animals as they would library books, there was some evidence that the creatures benefited as well as the children themselves. The children learned how to feed and care for them.

Creatures are often brought to the classroom where the child learns responsibility in caring for a pet, gains insight into ways adults care for him/her, and grows in self-confidence as he/she assumes care of the pet.

Animals or pets provide a variety of subjects for discussion that open the door to communication.

Five Little Puppies

L.B.S.

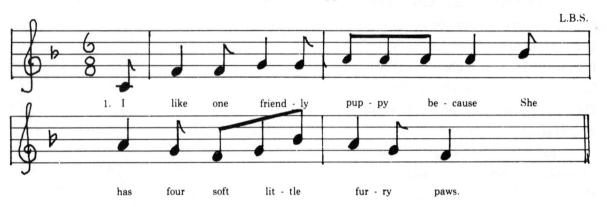

1. I like one friendly puppy because
   She has four soft little furry paws.

2. The reason I like two puppies is that
   Their bodies are little and round and fat.

3. I like three puppies because they're fun.
   They play with me as they jump and run.

4. My four puppies bark when I say, "Hello!"
   They follow me wherever I go.

5. Five puppies are sleepy and new and small.
   They are so friendly—I love them all.

(Use as a finger play as the song is sung, or children volunteer and one at a time form a line.)

170

Pets in Our Classroom

One white rabbit came to our classroom.

And she stayed only one day.

We fed her lettuce and carrots.

It's too bad she couldn't stay.

Two hamsters came to our classroom.

They filled their little cheeks

With vegetables and lots of fruit,

And they made sharp little squeaks.

Three caterpillars came to our classroom.

They stayed, but by and by,

One day we went to look at them,

Each was a butterfly!

Four canaries came to our classroom.

And for us they did sing.

They made great entertainment,

As we watched them swing.

Five fish came to our classroom.

They were quite a lively brood.

We liked to watch them swim around

And dart up for their food.

Six turtles came to our classroom,

In a terrarium.

It had warm water and a rock.

Good pets they did become.

Seven lizards came to our classroom.

They needed a terrarium, too.

They ate all kinds of insects,

And gave us quite a view.

Eight red ants came to our classroom,

In a box of glass.

We fed them drops of honey.

They were fun to have in class.

So we have had some visitors,

And each one was a pet.

If you could have a choice of them,

Now which one would you get?

(Use as a finger play. Children hold up designated number of fingers. Pause for a discussion of each animal, bird, or insect. Read these books to the class: Fish Is Fish *by Leo Lionni; Pantheon Books, New York, 1970 and* The Very Hungry Caterpillar *by Eric Carle; Collins-World, New York, 1967.)*

Little Ants

One little ant, two little ants,

Three little ants I see.

Four little ants, five little ants,

Lively as can be.

Six little ants, seven little ants,

Eight in a bowl of glass.

Nine little ants, ten little ants

Entertain our class.

(Many children enjoy ant villages. Red ants make good classroom pets. Recommended reading: The Ants Go Marching *by Berniece Freschel; Charles Scribner's Sons, New York, 1973 and* Ants Don't Get Sunday Off *by Penny Pollock; Putnam, New York, 1978.)*

(Point to a finger each time.)

Canary Pets at School

One yellow canary sings to its mate.

When we are trying to concentrate.

Two yellow canaries warble a tune

Before we go home in the afternoon.

Three yellow canaries ask for a seed

When I am trying to write and read.

Four yellow canaries swing to and fro.

They chirp and they leap and they make quite a show.

Five yellow canaries—I watch them all hop.

Soon they'll go back to the canary shop.

The pet shop lent them, and so now you know.

We will be so sorry to see them go.

(Hold up one finger, then two, three, and so on.)

Six Little Fish

Six little fish, two in each pair,

Coming up occasionally for a breath of air.

Two swim up, and two swim down;

They swim in a circle around and around.

Six come up.

They swim by threes.

But whenever I feed them, they don't say please.

Six little fish swim around, around.

They play tag with each other

And never make a sound.

(Hold up six fingers.)
(Hold up three fingers on each hand.)

(This rhyme can teach the beginning of multiplication: 2 × 3 = 6 or 3 × 2 = 6. Discuss the meaning of the word pair: *pair of ears, hands, eyes, feet, legs, shoulders and arms. Suggest that the children draw and cut out fish from yellow construction paper which will stick to the flannelboard, if it is tilted slightly backward. Show a pair of fish. Show two swimming up and two swimming down. Show six in two sets of three each. Join the two sets to make six fish. Read the rhyme aloud several times and it will be easy to learn by rote.)*

Wiggling Puppies

One little puppy, one

Wiggled his tail and had wiggling fun.   (Wiggle finger.)

Two little puppies, two

Wiggled their bodies as puppies do.   (Wiggle whole self.)

Three little puppies, three

Wiggled their noses happily.   (Move nose.)

Four little puppies, four

Wiggled their shoulders and wiggled some more.   (Move shoulders.)

Five little puppies fat and round,

Wiggled their ears when they heard a sound.

(This rhyme will be easy for children to learn. Choose five children who join a set, one at a time, as the rhyme is dramatized.)

Five Black Kittens

Five black kittens stayed up late   (Hold up five fingers.)

Sitting on top of the garden gate.

The stars came out and the moon did, too.   (Wiggle fingers; make circle for moon.)

The five little kittens began to mew.   (Show five fingers.)

Along came the mother with a lovely purr   (Move thumb of opposite hand toward kittens.)

And she took the kittens back home with her.

Three Fat Kittens

Three fat kittens were playing in the sun.   (Point to one finger at a time.)

This one saw a rabbit and she began to run.

This one saw a beetle and she began to chase.

This one say a butterfly and she began to race.

Three fat kittens chased their tails

And they went round and round   (Children turn around.)

Three fat kittens went to sleep   (Children sink slowly to floor and relax.)

And made a purring sound.

Turtle Decisions

Said turtle one to turtle two,

"What do you think we ought to do?"

Said turtle two to turtle three,

"Do you think that we can all agree?"

Said turtle three to turtle four,

"Shall we creep along as we did before?"

Said turtle four to turtle five,

"Shall we rest beside that big beehive?"

The five turtles couldn't make a decision,

So they all went home to watch television!

(Ask, "What do you think about turtles that never could make up their minds? How would you advise those turtles? How could you help them decide what to do?" Recommended reading: Turtle Pond *by Berniece Freschel; Charles Scribner's Sons, New York, 1971, and* Rosebud *by Ed Emberley; Little, Brown and Co., Boston, 1966.)*

I Saw Two Cats

I saw two cats, two, two, two.

And each cat said, "Mew, mew, mew."

Another cat made three, three, three.

I wish they were for me, me, me.

Another cat made four, four, four.

But still I wanted more, more, more.

I took them home, but sakes alive!

I found that I had five, five, five.

My mama said, "That's fine, fine, fine."

So all five cats are mine, mine, mine.

(A fourth grade child who is still mastering English as a second language wrote this delightful rhyme, which she has taught her young brothers and sisters to play at home.)

Five Gray Cats

Five little cats all soft and gray

Had five balls of yarn with which to play.   (Use anything round.)

Each cat had two ears on her velvety head.   (Point to ears.)

And a voice that purred gently when she was fed.

Each little cat had two bright eyes,   (Point to eyes.)

174

And a furry tail of ENORMOUS size. (Measure length.)

Each little cat had four white paws. (Ask how many paws there would be altogether for all cats.)

Each paw in the front had five sharp claws. (Hold up five fingers on each hand.)

Each cat had a tongue to lap up milk. (Show tongue.)

Each cat had a coat as smooth as silk. (Stroke arm.)

Look! How many cats do you see? (Response.)

How many balls of yarn will there be? (Response.)

How many paws do you see there? (Ten.)

How many tails to wave in the air? (Play a triangle as children count.)

How many mice run across the floor? (Choose any number to do this.)

How many mice hide behind the door? (Chose any number beforehand.)

(Recommended reading: A. Birnbaum, Green Eyes; *Western Publishing Company, New York, 1953, and Franz Brandenberg,* A Robber! A Robber!; *Greenwillow, New York, 1976.)*

Three Furry Kittens

The first furry kitten

Found an old shoe.

The second kitten crept inside,

And so there were _____.

The second furry kitten

Climbed up a tree.

A third kitten joined her,

And then there were _____.

Three furry kittens

Sat beside my door.

I fed them food till they were full,

And still they asked for more.

(Bring in a young kitten for one day. Discuss its behavior with the class. They watch the kitten drink milk and sleep.)

Cats Asleep

When all of my cats are asleep in the sun,

I like to count them one by one.

The first is Candy so cunning and sweet. (Point to each of four fingers.)

The second is Captain who looks so neat.

The third is Cotton with cuddly fur.

The fourth is Cubby with happy purr.

When all of my cats are asleep in the sun.

I like to count them one by one.

(Ask children to name the fifth, sixth, seventh, eighth cats, etc. They may cut pictures of cats from magazines and mount them in a row on a sheet of poster paper or back with flannel for the flannelboard.)

My Pets

There are a lot of pets in my house.

I have one gerbil and one white mouse.   (Hold up one finger on each hand.)

I have two kittens and two green frogs   (Hold up two fingers on each hand.)

I have three goldfish and three big dogs.   (Hold up three fingers on each hand.)

Some folks say that is a lot!

Tell how many pets I've got.   (Twelve.)

(You may make marks on the chalkboard for the numbers of pets and at the end children count them. Encourage a discussion on pets: what they like to eat, where they sleep, and so on. Write number sentences on the board: One plus one equals two, and so on.)

Goldfish Pets

One little goldfish

Lives in a bowl.

Two little goldfish

Eat their food whole.

Three little goldfish

Swim all around.

Although they move,

They don't make a sound.

Four little goldfish

Have swishy tails.

Five little goldfish

Have pretty scales.

(Suggest that children cut fishes from yellow construction paper and lay them on the flannelboard. If the board is slanted slightly backward the fish will cling. Children may add one "fish" at a time and count as they do so.)

Two Little Turtles

One little turtle lived in a shell,

And that was a home

That he liked very well.   (Make back out of hand.)

He poked out his head   (Thumb protrudes between middle finger and forefinger.)

To look at the view.

Another turtle joined him   (Thumb protrudes between middle finger and forefinger on other hand.)

And that made two.

They had small tails,

Their feet made tracks,   (Wiggle fingers.)

And both of the turtles carried homes on their backs.

MEADOW AND STREAM

The Animals

I saw one hungry little mouse.

Squeak, squeak, squeak!

I said, "There's cheese inside my house."

Squeak, squeak, squeak!

I saw two funny little moles.

Creep, creep, creep!

I said, "I'll help you dig your holes

Deep, deep, deep!"

I saw three frogs beside three logs.

Glug, glug, glug!

I fed some bugs to the hungry frogs.

Glug, glug, glug!

Four little fish swam with a swish.

Glip, glip, glup!

I fed some seaweed to the fish.

Glip, glip, glup!

I said, "Here rabbits, come and eat."

Nibble, nibble, nibble.

I fed five rabbits carrots sweet.

Nibble, nibble, nibble.

Six butterflies said, "Come and fly."

Flutter, flutter, fly!

I went to fly with the butterflies.

Flutter, flutter, fly!

(Children point to designated number of fingers and say the animal's sound or refrain. Encourage verbal participation. Read Over in the Meadow *by Ezra Jack Keats; Scholastic, New York, 1957.)*

Three Old Rats

Three old rats went out to dine

In tails and top hats dressed up fine.

The first rat said, "Yum! Yum! A cupcake!"

The second rat said, "I've a tummyache."

The third rat said, "Oh, mercy me!

Lunch is over and it's time for tea!"

(Children volunteer for parts and say the lines in quotation marks as the class says the other lines. They may sit at a table and dramatize the action. Encourage them to draw pictures of the rats.)

Mouse in the House

Five little mice ran around the house.

Four mice hid and that left one mouse.

One little mouse peeked behind the door.

Four little mice came back to the floor.

Two little mice ran behind a tree.

They stayed right there, and that left three.

(Wiggle fingers.)

(Hold up one finger.)

(Insert pointer finger between two fingers of opposite hand.)

(Wiggle five fingers again.)

(Clasp two fingers.)

(Bend down ring and small fingers.)

Three little mice didn't like where they'd been,

So five little mice got together again.   (Hold up five fingers.)

*(Five children form a set on the rug and leave or
return to the set as the poem dictates.)*

Three Little Fish

Three little fish were swimming in a pool.

"Come," said the mother, "It is time to go to   (Beckon with finger.)
school.

Learn to nibble seaweed and learn to swim   (Motion of swimming; hand moves back and
around,   forth.)

And learn to dive from pussycats that make a   (Pull fingers in and out beside face to simulate
"F,f' sound!"   whiskers.)

Ten Toads

Ten brown toads hopped in a line.

One slipped away and that left _____.   (Children supply number.)

Nine toads went to investigate.   (Bend down one finger at a time.)

One forgot where he was and that left _____.

Eight toads went on a hopping spree to Devon

One strayed far away, and that left _____.

Seven brown toads were visiting Fort Dix.

One fell off the jeep, and that left _____.

Six brown toads did a jumping jive.

One jumped up too high, and that left _____.

Five brown toads were sitting by a door

One ran away, and that left _____.

Four brown toads were resting near a tree.

One fell in a rabbit hutch, and that left _____.

Three brown toads were blinking in the sun.

All woke up and jumped away and that left

_____.

*(Say, "Make up a story about something the last
three toads did. What did the first and second
toads do?")*

Ten Little Mice

Ten little mice went out to play,   *Continue the rhyme until only one mouse re-
                                                mains. End the rhyme in this way:*
Picking up bread crumbs along the way.

Along came a tomcat sleek and black,   One little mouse went out to play

And only nine little mice came back.   Picking up bread crumbs along the way.

Tomcat chased but he couldn't catch one;

So all of the ten little mice ran home.

(A rug may serve as a set. Ten children sit on the rug, leaving one at a time. Each time a mouse leaves, write the remaining number on the board in large numerals. When the last mouse leaves, say "This is the empty set. Not one mouse is in the set.")

Five Little Polliwogs

Five little polliwogs swam near the shore.

The first one said, "I have been this way before."

The second one said, "I have a funny tail."

The third one said, "And a tail can help me sail."

The fourth one said, "My legs are getting strong."

The fifth one said, "It will not be very long."

The five little polliwogs deep down in the bog

Gave three croaks and each one became a frog.

(Discuss how a polliwog turns into a frog. Sing the songs "Three Little Polliwogs" and "Three Little Speckled Frogs" from More Singing Fun *by Lucille F. Wood and Louise Binder Scott; Bowmar/Noble, Los Angeles, 1954.)*

(Hold up five fingers.)

(Point to each finger as a tadpole is mentioned.)

Five Little Tadpoles

Five little tadpoles went for a swim.

The first little tadpole put his head in.

The second little tadpole put his head back

The third little tadpole dived for a snack.

The fourth little tadpole with his tiny brother,

Went out to look for his father and mother.

(Review ordinals. Ask, "What is a snack? When you eat a snack, what do you have to eat? Have you ever seen a tadpole? Where? Is it always a tadpole? What happens to it?" Discuss how a tadpole turns into a frog.)

Four Young Frogs

Four young frogs were swimming in a pond.

Of little green flies they were very, very fond.

The first frog croaked with a glug, glug, glug,

"I wish I could find a fly or a bug."

The second frog said, "Oh, I am very wise,

Because I have such great big eyes!"

The third frog said, "Oh, I see a fly!

It seems to be flying very close by."

The fourth frog gave an ENORMOUS yawn,

And snap, the little green fly was gone.

(Hold up four fingers.)

The four frogs had a good lunch that day.

They jumped in the pond and they all swam
away.

*(This is a review of ordinals - first, second, third,
and fourth. Write the numerals on the board.
Dramatize the poem or use as a finger play.)*

Five Little Frogs

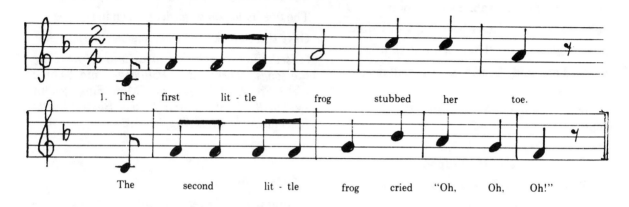

1. The first little frog stubbed her toe.
   The second little frog cried, "Oh, oh, oh!"

2. The third little frog said, "There, there,
   Here is a bug that I will share."

3. The fourth little frog came along
   And sang a special get-well song.

4. The fifth little frog looked so hard
   To find a friendly greeting card.

5. The first little frog stubbed her toe.
   But that was a long, long time ago.

6. She hops and hops with all of her friends,
   And that is all. Our story ends.

*(Review the ordinals as the story is dramatized.
Children volunteer to play the frogs.)*

A Little Green Frog

A little green frog in a pond am I.

Hoppity, hoppity, hop!

I sit on a leaf that is high and dry.

Hoppity, hoppity, hop!

I watch all the fish as they swim by.

Hoppity, hoppity, hop!

SPLASH! How I make the water fly!

Hoppity, hoppity, SPLASH!

(Read Allynn's Polliwog *by Ann and Harlow Rockwell; Doubleday, Garden City, New York, 1970.)*

(Children say refrain.)

This Little Bunny

This little bunny has pink eyes.

This little bunny is very wise.

This little bunny is soft as silk.

This little bunny is white as milk.

This little bunny nibbles away

At cabbages and carrots the live-long day.

(Hold up fingers one at a time. Make rabbit ears for the children from white construction paper and line ears with pink paper. Cut a strip of paper, fold it in the center and insert the ears. Glue them in the fold. Fasten around the child's head using a paper fastener. Read Seven Little Rabbits *by John Becker; Scholastic, New York, 1973, and* Mr. Rabbit and the Lovely Presents *by Charlotte Zolotow; Harper and Row, New York, 1966.)*

Ten Green Frogs

Ten green frogs were sitting on a well.

One leaned over and down he fell.

Reach up high. Bend down low.

Now only nine frogs are sitting in a row.

Children sit in a circle or row. One at a time leaves the group. End the rhyme in this way:

One green frog was sitting on a well.

He leaned over and down he fell.

Reach up high. Bend down low.

And now no frogs are sitting in a row.

Five Little Squirrels

Five little squirrels lived up in a tree.	(Hold up five fingers.)
And they were alike as squirrels could be.	
The first little squirrel was alone one day.	(Point to one finger at a time.)
He called to his friends, "Come on and play!"	
The second little squirrel jumped down from a limb.	
The first little squirrel jumped after him.	
The third little squirrel found nuts to eat.	
He cracked them and oh, they tasted sweet.	
The fourth little squirrel played hide and seek.	
She hid her eyes and she did not peek.	
The fifth little squirrel called, "Chirr-chirr-chirr-eeee,"	
And all of the squirrels came back to the tree.	(Hold up five fingers.)

Five Little Bunnies

Five little bunnies are such dears!	
The first little bunny has pink ears.	(Hold up a finger at each side of head.)
The second little bunny has soft toes.	(Point to feet.)
The third little bunny sniffs with her nose.	(Make two sniffs.)
The fourth little bunny is very smart.	(Point to forehead.)
The fifth little bunny has a loving heart.	(Place hand over heart.)

(This rhyme will help children to understand ordinal numbers. It can be used as a finger play or acted out. After a second or third reading, the class will be able to say much of the rhyme with you. Ask them to supply rhyming words, stopping just before the word. Recommended reading: Listen Rabbit *by Aileen Fisher; Thomas Y. Crowell, New York, 1964, and* The Country Bunny and the Little Gold Shoes *by Dubose Hayward; Houghton-Mifflin, Boston, 1939.)*

Five Furry Chipmunks

Five furry chipmunks	
We simply adore.	
One hid behind a branch,	
Then there were ———.	(Children supply missing number.)
Four furry chipmunks	
Were climbing up a tree.	
One slid to the ground,	

Then there were _____.
Three furry chipmunks
Found an old shoe.
One crawled inside of it,
Then there were _____.
Two furry chipmunks
Were chasing in the sun.
One got tired and rested,
Then there were _____.
One furry chipmunk
Wanted to run—so,
ABRACADABRA!
Then there was _____.

This is the Squirrel

This is the squirrel
   that lives in a tree.
This is the tree
   that she climbs.
This is the nut
   that she takes from me
When I sit very still
   sometimes!

(Using climbing motion, make a circle of fingers for nut. Fold hands on last line.)

Baby Porcupine

Little baby porcupine,
What is on your back?
They are quills and every quill
Is sharper than a tack.
(Hold up ten fingers for quills.)

Five Busy Honey Bees

Five busy honey bees were resting in the sun.
The first one said, "Let us have some fun."
The second one said, "Where shall it be?"
The third one said, "Up in the honey tree."
The fourth one said, "Let's make some honey sweet."
The fifth one said, "With pollen on our feet."
The five little busy bees sang their buzzing tune,
As they worked in the beehive all that afternoon.
   Bzzzzzzz!   Bzzzzzzzz!

(Use as a finger play or a dramatization with five children each saying a line. The class says the lines not in quotations and everyone buzzes.)

SIX-LEGGED CREATURES

Insects are an important part of everything in this world. Scientists believe that perhaps four million species of insects exist on this planet and as many are unknown as are known. Some are so tiny that they could walk through the eye of a needle.

Young children benefit from a study of insects. The tiny species whet the curiosity, encourage observation skills, foster an appreciation for all forms of life, increase vocabulary, and provide practical information. Children are most likely to identify with moths, butterflies, beetles, fireflies, ladybugs, red and black ants, crickets, and grasshoppers.

Harmful insects should be discussed: fleas and mosquitos that bite, hornets that sting, lice that inhabit bodies, tomato bugs that harm crops, and termites which destroy property. Children, of course, realize that many insects are useful. The bee provides honey, insects are food for animals, predators devour harmful ones, and ladybugs eat aphids that demolish orange crops.

Children are fascinated by the life cycle as well as the structure of the insects. A terrarium can be provided where silk worms can be raised and ant villages displayed.

Insects appeal to the child's imagination. Often they relate the tiny creatures to their own feelings. One child remarked, "The ants are proud when they do good work." They may ask, "How does the cricket feel when the weather is cold? Is its music sad or happy?" One child said, "Ladybugs look like newly painted cars."

Six Little Beetles

Six little beetles liked to play.	(Hold up six fingers.)
Two little beetles scampered away.	
Only four little beetles were left to play.	(Hold up four fingers.)
Four little beetles began to race.	
Two little beetles left the place.	
So two little beetles were left that day.	(Hold up two fingers.)
Two little beetles were left to play.	
Two little beetles got a drink.	
Two little beetles left, I think.	(Place fingers behind back.)
Six little beetles said, "We'd rather	
That all of us beetles got back together."	(Show six fingers again.)

184

Five Pretty Butterflies

Children: Flittery-flutter, the color of butter.

Flittery-flutter across the blue sky.

Fluttery-flutter, their golden wings glitter,

Beautiful butterflies fluttering by.

Child 1: One pretty butterfly fluttered and flew.

Child 2: Another one joined her and then there were two.

Children: (Repeat refrain.)

Child 3: Two pretty butterflies sat in a tree.

Child 4: They called their first cousin and then there were three.

Children: (Repeat refrain.)

Child 5: Three pretty butterflies flew near my door.

Child 6: Along came another and then there were four.

Children: (Repeat refrain.)

Child 7: Four pretty butterflies, when they arrived,

Child 8: Sent for their sister, and then there were five.

Children: (Repeat refrain.)

(The children may want to make up a tune for the refrain. Type lines for individual children if they can read. Otherwise, tell them what to say and line them up horizontally. The entire class may say or sing the refrain.)

New Butterfly

On a milkweed leaf,

Here is a cocoon.   (Cup hands.)

Something is happening.

Will it be soon?   (Peek inside cupped hands.)

Oh, it is coming

With wings folded so.

Now they are spreading.   (Spread arms.)

Ready to go.

Look at the green and gold

Butterfly!

Fly away! Fly away! And good-bye!   (Children "fly" to seats.)

185

The Bugs Go Marching

The bugs go marching one by one.

The little one stopped to wiggle its thumb.

They all go marching once again   (Refrain.)

Go marching to escape the rain.

The bugs go marching two by two.

The little one stopped to tie its shoe.

They all go marching once again,   (Refrain.)

Go marching to escape the rain.

The bugs go marching three by three.

The little one stopped to disagree.

They all go marching once again,   (Refrain.)

Go marching to escape the rain.

Continue with:

The bugs go marching four by four.

The little one stopped to shut the door.

The bugs go marching five by five.

The little one stopped to learn to drive.

The bugs go marching six by six.

The little one stopped to do some tricks.

The bugs go marching seven by seven.

The little one stopped to point to heaven.

The bugs go marching eight by eight.

The little one stopped to shut the gate.

The bugs go marching nine by nine.

The little one stopped to walk a line.

The bugs go marching, ten by ten.

The little one stopped to say, "THE END."

-Traditional

(Start with two children, adding two more each time until there are "ten by ten." The one at the end of a line stops for the action and all then stop. They begin again as the lines are repeated and new bugs are added. The class may choose one "bug" to perform the action. One can be chosen to say, "The End.")

Crickets

There's a noisy little cricket
That's as lively as can be.
There's a noisy little cricket
And he always sings to me.
There's a noisy little cricket,
And when everything is still.
That noisy little cricket,
Sings beneath my window sill.
One more cricket comes along   (Hold up a finger for each cricket.)
And helps the cricket with his song.

Two noisy little crickets
Are as lively as can be.
Two noisy little crickets,
And they always sing to me.
Two noisy little crickets,
And when everything is still,
Two noisy little crickets sing
Beneath my window sill.
One more cricket comes along
And helps the crickets with their song.

(Continue the rhyme with as many children as desired. Children say refrain - "_____ more cricket comes along and helps the crickets with their song" - each time. Children can be chosen to represent crickets and one at a time move to a circle drawn on the floor or to a rug. One child can play an autoharp as the rhyme is said. The rest of the children can imitate crickets.)

This Little Cricket

The first little cricket played a violin.   (Point to one finger at a time.)
The second little cricket joined right in.
The third little cricket made a crackly song.
The fourth little cricket helped him along.
The fifth little cricket cried, "Crick-crick-cree.
The orchestra is over and it's time for tea!"

The Wedding

All:	Ding-ding-a-dong!
	Let's sing a song.
Child 1:	The bells in the steeple
Child 2:	Are calling the people.
All:	Come, come, come!
	A wedding's begun!
	Ding-ding-a-dong!
	Ding-ding-a-dong!
Child 3:	Who's getting married?
Child 4:	Why, can't you see?
Child 5:	The ant is marrying the bumble bee!
All:	Ding-a-ding-dong!
	Let's sing a song.
	Come, come, come!
	The wedding's begun!

(Children clap.)

(Use for choral speaking.)

The Ladybugs

Tick-tack-tick-tack! See them go!

Four little ladybugs are marching in a row. (Hold up four fingers.)

The first one is yellow and trimmed with specks of black. (Point to one finger at a time.)

The second one is orange with a round and shiny back.

The third one is bright red with teeny, tiny dots.

The fourth one is fancy with different kinds of spots.

Ladybugs help ranchers. Ladybugs have use.

They eat up all the orange tree pests,

So we can have orange juice!

Animals and Insects

Here is an ostrich straight and tall (Arms above head with wrist bent forward for ostrich's head.)

Nodding her head above us all.

Here is a bullsnake on the ground, (Move hand back and forth.)

Wiggling around with a hissing sound.

Here is an eagle flying high (Spread arms and move like wings.)

And spreading his wings across the sky.

Here is a porcupine with quills on back.

Each quill is sharper than a sharp tack.

Here is a spider upon the gate.   (Spread five fingers behind fist on other hand.)

I counted its legs and there were eight.   (Hold up eight fingers.)

Here is an owl with great round eyes   (Circle eyes with fingers.)

And here are some flickering fireflies.   (Wiggle fingers.)

Ant under a Plant

Ant, ant, under a plant.

How many legs have you?

One, two, three, four, five, and six.   (Count fingers.)

I thought you always knew.

You have two feet. You have two legs.   (Hold up two fingers.)

I have four more legs than you.   (Hold up four fingers.)

(Write these number sentences: Four plus two equals six. Six minus two is four. Six minus four is two.)

The Little Caterpillars

Ten little caterpillars crawled up on a vine.

One slipped off and out of sight, and then there were _____.

Nine little caterpillars sat upon the gate.

One hid behind the latch, and then there were _____.

Eight little caterpillars in a row quite even.

One went to find a leaf, and then there were _____.

Seven little caterpillars tried to find some sticks.

One went behind a bush, and then there were _____.

Six little caterpillars crawled down the drive.

One skittled far away, and then there were _____.

Five little caterpillars were creeping as before.

One slipped inside a crack, and then there were _____.

Four little caterpillars climbed up a tree.

One hid behind some bark, and then there were _____.

Three little caterpillars found leaves that were new.

One crawled far out of sight and then there were _____.

Two little caterpillars were snoozing in the sun.

One woke up and dashed away, and then there was _____.

One little caterpillar, before the set of sun,

Turned into a butterfly and then there was _____.

(The children supply the remaining number each time. Call attention to phrases: "There were _____" and "There was _____." Use them in sentences so that children can understand these tenses. After ten children have had a turn, choose ten more. The selection can also be used as a finger play with all children in the class bending down fingers. Read The Very Hungry Caterpillar *by Eric Carle; Collins-World, New York, 1969.)*

Ten Little Grasshoppers

Ten little grasshoppers were swinging on a vine.

One ate too many grapes and then there were nine.

Nine little grasshoppers were sitting on the gate.

One blew far, far away and then there were eight.

Eight little grasshoppers were flying up toward heaven.

One got lost in a cloud, and then there were sevven.

Seven little grasshoppers hid between two bricks.

One thought that he must leave, and so there were six.

Six little grasshoppers were glad to be alive;

One chased a bumblebee, and then there were five.

Five little grasshoppers were leaping on the floor.

One hid inside a crack, then there were four.

Four little grasshoppers saw a tiny flea,

One tried to catch it and then there were three.

Three little grasshoppers said, "What shall we do?"

One skipped merrily away, and then there were two.

Two little grasshoppers were dancing in the sun;

One hid behind a bush, and then there was one.

One little grasshopper was left to have his fun.

He leaped away to join his friends, and then there were none.

(Bend down fingers one at a time. The rhyme can be acted out by ten children. Read The Butterfly Ball and the Grasshopper Feast *by William Rosco, pictures by Don Bologness; McGraw-Hill, New York, 1967.)*

TRAVEL BY LAND, SEA, AND AIR

Travel

The pioneers of long ago
  Had no T.V. or radio,
    Or telephone or streamlined train,
      Or motor boat or fast jet plane.

In covered wagons they would go;
  And oxen travel was quite slow.
    We travel now by land and sea
      Ships take us where we want to be.

Large airplanes fly us through the air.
  Trains bring livestock and clothes we wear.
    The big trucks rumble down the street,
      And bring us vegetables and meat.

Today, folks travel on paved roads,
  The buses carry heavy loads.
    Yes, travel takes us many ways
      By land, by sea, and air these days.

And who knows? Maybe very soon,
  We'll be transported to the moon!

Wheels

Wheels, wheels, wheels go around, around   (Twirl hands.)
Bicycles need wheels to move along the ground.
Are wheels ever square? No, they are round.   (Circle with hands.)
Wheels, wheels, wheels go around, around.   (Twirl hands again.)
(Suggest that individuals draw circles and ask the class to guess what they are going to make.)

Rocket Ship

Our rocket ship is standing by   (Hold up one finger.)
And very, very soon,
We'll have a count down, then we'll blast
Ourselves up to the moon.
Begin to count: ten, nine, eight,   (Count backward, bending down each finger.)
Be on time, don't be late.
Seven, six, five, and four,
There aren't many seconds more.
Three, two, one! Zero! Zip!
The rocket is off on its first moon trip.

I'm a Plane

I'm a plane with wings so bright   (Stoop and spread arms.)
Waiting here to take a flight.   (Rise slowly.)
Now I sail up straight and high.   (Stand with arms at sides.)
Now I sail around the sky.   (Turn body around.)
Now I land upon the ground,   (Sit.)
With a very quiet sound.
(This rhyme can also be used for relaxation.)

Three Astronauts

One astronaut climbs up the stair
To the capsule hatch which we see there.
Two astronauts sit side by side.
Three astronauts prepare for the ride.
The first one says, "We have checked controls."
The second one says, "We will reach our goals."
The third one says, "Turn the oxygen on."
All three says, "We will soon be gone."
The first one says, "We have checked things well.
Our system is working. We can tell."
The second one says, "I hear the motor sound.
Our ship is lifting off of the ground."
The third one says, "We are high in the sky.
We are already ten miles high."
Three astronauts sit quietly in place
All at their work in outer space.

(Volunteers become the astronauts. Write on slips of paper what each one is to say. They may make a ship from building blocks. Make space helmets from plastic water jugs. Cut off the bottom and front part from the forehead on down. Cover the edges with tape. Children can glue on buttons or items from the odds and ends box. Use a felt-tip pen for drawing or writing on the helmet.)

Ten Little Tugboats

Ten little tugboats are out on the sea

And that is where little tugboats should be.

Ten little tugboats got along fine,

Till one drifted far away, and then there were
_____.

Nine little tugboats said, "We can't wait."

One went too far out, and then there were
_____.

Eight little tugboats were lined up quite even.

One couldn't keep the pace, and then there were
_____.

Seven little tugboats, before you could say "ticks,"

One got lost in the fog and then there were
_____.

Six little tugboats had a lot of drive.

But one tooted out to sea, and then there were
_____.

Five little tugboats said, "Let's move to shore."

But one backed up from the rest, and then there were _____.

Four little tugboats were sailing evenly.

One hit a big barge, and then there were _____.

Three little tugboats said, "We'll carry through."

But one lost its engine, and then there were
_____.

Two little tugboats said, "We'll make the run."

But one lost its smokestack, and then there was
_____.

One little tugboat pulled a ship to shore.

That tugboat was successful, and now there are no more.

(Ask, "What is a tugboat supposed to do? What does successful *mean? How can someone be successful?" The children supply the number remaining each time.)*

The Airplane

The airplane has big wide wings.

Its propeller spins around and sings.

Vvvvvvvvv!

(Arms outstretched.)

(Make one arm go around.)

(Children make the continuous sound each time.)

The airplane goes up in the sky.

Then down it goes, just see it fly!

Vvvvvvvv!

(Lift arms up and then down.)

Up, up, and up; down, down, and down

Over every housetop in our town!

Vvvvvvvv!

(Continuous up and down action.)

The Family Car

Sometimes I ride in the family car.

The engine jerks so we cannot go far.

Pop, pop, pop, pop, pop, pop, pop!   (Children repeat.)

Pop, pop, pop! Juggle, jiggle, JAT.   (Children repeat.)

What is the matter?

Why, the tire is flat! Ssssssssssss!   (Children make sound.)

MAKE-BELIEVE

The Way to Make-Believe

Do you know the way to make-believe?

I'll tell you just right.

Wait till a yellow moon comes up

Over purple seas at night,

And makes a shining pathway

That is sparkling and bright.

Then if you know the very words

To cast a spell at night,

You'll get upon a thistledown,

And if the breeze is right,

You'll sail away to make-believe

Along this track of light!

The Pixies Have Tea

Five little Pixies decided to have tea

Beside a sparkling brooklet, beneath a willow tree.

The first one filled some acorn cups with a lovely morning dew.

The second brought some seeds of sesame to chew.

The third little Pixie put some cream and sugar in.

The fourth one tied a dainty napkin underneath her chin.

The fifth one brought a loaf of bread no bigger than your thumb.

The Pixies sang a Pixie song and were so glad they'd come.

(Suggest that the children draw pictures of Pixies. Ask, "Would a Pixie's food be like your food? What else might they have for tea? Would you like to have tea with the Pixies? Why? What kind of song would they sing? Can we make up a Pixie song? Tell more about what Pixies do." Explain that Pixies are fairies. You may use the rhyme as a finger play.)

194

Five Little Leprechauns

Five little leprechauns were dancing on the shore.

The king waved a magic wand, and then there were _____.

Four little leprechauns were dancing merrily.

The king waved a magic wand, and then there were _____.

Three little leprechauns danced a jig as they can do.

The king waved a magic wand, and then there were _____.

Two little leprechauns were dancing on the run.

The king waved a magic wand, and then there were _____.

One little leprechaun was lonely as could be.

The king called the leprechauns and gave them cakes and tea.

(The children supply the remaining number each time. Five children at a time may play the "story" rhyme and leave the set one at a time.)

A St. Patrick's Elf

I met a little elfman once,	
He wore a stovepipe hat.	(Place elf's green hat on flannelboard.)
His face was round and mischievous.	(Place face under hat.)
He stopped awhile to chat.	
I asked, "Why are your trousers green?	(Place trousers on board.)
Instead of red or blue?	
Your coat is green and there I see	(Place coat on board.)
A buckle on each shoe."	(Place two shoes on board.)
I asked, "What are you doing here?"	
And then I heard him say:	
"Why, I have come to visit you	
This fine St. Patrick's Day.	
I'm dressed in green from head to toe,	
For I'm an Irish elf.	
I wear a buckle on each shoe	
Which I made by myself."	
He said, "I've come to visit you	

Five Flying Saucer Men

Five flying saucer men were sitting on the stars.

Number one said, "Let's fly over to Mars."

Number two said, "I see rockets in the air."

Number three said, "Why should we care?"

Number four said, "So now let's say good-by."

Number five said, "Let's fly high in the sky."

SWISH went the saucer and on went the light,

And the five flying saucer men whizzed out of sight.

(Point to each finger as the rhyme is said. Change to first, second, third, fourth, and fifth if you wish to review ordinals. Make a flying saucer by stapling two foil pie tins together and adding antennae cut from foil.)

This fine St. Patrick's Day."

He sang a song and danced a jig,

And skipped far, far away.

(Read the poem aloud before any action is taken. Say, "Think of a St. Patrick's song the elf might have sung. Paint a picture of him. Help me make the parts of him for the flannelboard. Show how he would dance a jig." Cut all pieces from felt. Then you are ready to present the poem as children take turns placing the pieces on the flannelboard.)

Autumn Elves

Five little elves met one autumn day.	(Hold up five fingers.)
Five little elves decided they would play,	
And paint with rainbow colors.	
Each elf was in a rush	
To paint the leaves upon the trees	
With his own paint brush.	
The first little elf found a jar of red	(Hold up one finger.)
And painted the flowers in the flower bed.	
The second little elf shinnied up on a limb.	(Hold up two fingers.)
And found a green leaf that he could trim.	
The third little elf with a stroke of brown	(Hold up three fingers.)
Painted each leaf that came tumbling down.	
The fourth little elf was a happy fellow.	(Hold up four fingers.)
He found a leaf and painted it yellow.	
The fifth little elf painted all of the night.	(Hold up five fingers.)
Until his leaves were orange bright.	
Next day, people looked at the painted trees,	
And they felt a chill in the autumn breeze.	
But nobody thought of the little elves,	
1, 2, 3, 4, 5—all proud of themselves!	(Count on fingers.)

(This rhyme should be an encouragement to paint leaves. Ask the children to pretend to be elves, paint, cut out, and back their leaves with bits of flannel for the flannelboard to use for counting activities.)

EPILOGUE

Rhymes for Learning Times is designed for teacher, for parent, and for child involvement. It is a "plan" book and if used frequently it will ensure that a child is exposed to a wide range of concepts.

The rhymes are not intended for imitation only. If one considers the purposes described, he/she will note the warm encouragement which helps a young child to build a secure and satisfying self-image. The rhymes also foster linguistic development and reasoning power through interaction with others, and promote social cooperation among children upon which development of intellect depends.

The rhymes accentuate body movement and help develop large and small muscles. They emphasize spatial relationships, teach simple mathematics, and act as a form of relaxation which will give both child and teacher a sense of repose. They stimulate listening skills and help establish reading readiness. This book contains a number of foreign language rhymes which foster appreciation of other cultures and serve as a motivation for discussion and multi-cultural understanding. The rhymes offer opportunities for the less able child to work inconspicuously and independently and allow all children to perceive and eliminate emotional problems which cannot be verbalized.

Teachers will create the favorable environment to give as varied experience as possible and to stimulate the child's imagination, thinking and physical behavior. The environment must suit the child as well as the teacher or parent. Teachers and parents who wish to create an atmosphere of learning for their children will enter into the play "let's pretend" and become active participants. Adequate space must be provided so that children as a group can move freely and uninhibitedly. At the same time, teachers should be aware of their responsibilities in seeing that each child achieves certain learning goals.

Although one cannot look into a child's mind, to be an effective teacher or parent, one must study a child's learning processes and realize the degree of awareness that differs from child to child.

Before any goals can be accomplished through the use of action rhymes, the teacher and child must walk side by side. The selections in this book require a *feeling* for children, a *flexibility,* and an *alert observation* which waits for signals of readiness in order to help a child learn.

One must *be* a child to know rhythm which is the essence of life. As night follows day, as rest follows sleep, as work follows play, and as one heartbeat follows another, children experience rhythm when they turn, run, jump, twist, move fingers, sing, speak, or perform any of the activities in this book.

We can help children to preserve that priceless gift of rhythm and fantasy so that the enchantment of make-believe will continue throughout their lives.

It is hoped that this publication will give the teachers, parents, and the child, the enjoyment and satisfaction for which it is intended.

TITLE INDEX

SUBJECT INDEX
FOR UNIT INTEGRATION